CARIBBEAN HEAT

SEDUCTION SERIES BOOK ONE

RAE WINTERS

CARIBBEAN HEAT

Copyright © 2012 by Rae Winters

ISBN-13: 978-1475138191

ISBN-10: 1475138199

All rights reserved. No part of this book may be reproduced or transmitted in any form or by any means without written permission from the author.

This is a work of fiction. Characters, name, incidents organizations and dialogue in the novel are either products of the author's imagination or used fictitiously.

Printed in USA by CreateSpace

DEDICATION

A special thanks to my sister of the pen, Nathasha Brooks-Harris, for your love and support in bringing this book to life.

Enjoy this sample of my sensual poetry.

The Morning After

You woke up to my morning erection,
Knocking, wanting to come in for a visit,
but you resisted, playing shy and innocent.

My caress and commanding strokes,
lure you to my way of thinking.
Your trembling body, warm
and moist, electrified me.

Finally, you opened wide to welcome me inside,
sucking in all of me.
Our erotic ride was
Feverish—passionate—and memorable,
swept away by your touch.

Time stood still as we lay afresh
in the aftermath.
The afterglow of our intimacy
glistened between us.

The morning after.

Rae Winters © 2006

Chapter One

St. Lucia, West Indies, May 7, 2010

"Oooh Mike…yes, that's it, baby. Give it to me!" she cried out in her native French accent when Michael pulled out and thrusted back into her juicy ass.

Feverishly, Michael pumped into her high yellow ass as he palmed her jiggling melon-sized breasts riding her bareback.

Barefoot, Shay Bennett, slipped into her hotel room, at the Almond Morgan Bay Beach Resort ready to get something going with Michael. The room reeked of sex. Judging from the intensity of their moans and groans, they didn't even know Shay was there.

What the hell?!

Shay shook her head in disbelief. She couldn't believe she was watching Michael's ebony ass rapidly thrusting between that island slut's butt cheeks—in their resort's bed—as if they hadn't made love earlier that morning. He claimed he had a hangover and pleaded that he needed to lie down. The St. Lucian sun was too hot for him, and he wanted to stay inside of their air conditioned room to sleep off his headache. Shay ended up going down to the beach alone.

She found a secluded area next to the rocks, away from the mothers with their crying toddlers. Shay pulled up a lounge chair to get some sun. An hour later, perspiration beaded her face. Her orange string bikini stuck to her skin, and hot sand collected in the crack of her ass. Shay was melting out there, so she decided to join Michael in their room. Her intention was to slip right back into bed with him and give him a little something-something.

Damn, was she *pissed* to see Michael getting it on with the slut from The Pulse Club. The *same* woman she caught watching him the previous night.

Calm, but deadly as a cobra snake, she stepped over to the bed.

§

Michael bolted, flustered by Shay's sudden presence.

"S-Shay...Boo, this isn't what it looks like!" Michael stammered and pulled out of the woman. His cock was covered in her juices as he stood boldly.

Michael's afternoon delight dove under the sheets. Warily, her big brown eyes looked startled, like a deer caught in headlights. Her hair was standing on top of her head, revealing the tracks from a bad weave job.

I'll pull out every one of her tracks, Shay thought. *Michael betrays me with this woman, because I wouldn't give him anal sex.*

"Get out!" Shay hissed towering over her.

The bitch looked at Shay as if she didn't understand English.

"Don't act like you don't understand me! A few minutes ago, you spoke English very well: 'Oooh Mike. Yes, that's it, baby. Give it to me!'" Shay mimicked the trick's response to Michael taking her in the ass.

Then, Shay's calmness exploded. She grabbed the bitch's auburn-colored hair and yanked her out of the bed, but the weave broke off between Shay's fingers.

"Ouch, get off me!" the woman screamed.

Shay reached out for a thicker patch of hair and dragged her across the hardwood floor. Although the woman kicked and screamed, Shay's adrenaline was pumping high when she deposited the woman outside of the hotel room, followed by her maid's uniform. Then, she wheeled her cart out of the room.

"I will be contacting management about their lousy cleaning service!" Shay quipped.

She marched back into the room.

My funds paid for this romantic getaway, Shay thought.

"Get your nasty ass out of *my* room, Michael Powers!" She picked up Michael's suitcase. He hadn't unpacked yet, and she rolled it over to the door. She tossed it right out of the room, followed by his shirt and pants. The one he wore last evening.

The suitcase missed the woman by a mere inch. She quickly dressed, ignoring the sets of doors opening and the pairs of eyes looking out to see what the commotion was going on in the next room.

"Shay, let's discuss this." Michael ran over to her to stop her from tossing his cologne and personal toiletries, along with the rest of his things out of the room.

"Discuss *what*?" Shay laughed. "It's over, Michael!"

She ran over to the nightstand and picked up the telephone.

Michael tried to grab the phone out of Shay's hands.

"Don't-touch-me!" she hissed. Anger lit up her eyes.

Michael had one time considered Shay's hazel eyes as beautiful; but right then, they looked hostile as if she would hurt him. He backed away.

Shay pressed the button for the front desk.

"Hello…this is Shay Bennett, in room 205. I need to speak with the manager or the hotel security. I have an unwanted man in my room!" she said, throwing daggered looks at Michael.

A few seconds later, the call was transferred over.

"May I help you, ma'am?" a deep voice said across the phone line.

"Yes, I have a naked man in my room. I just found my man in bed fucking one of your hotel staff."

"Excuse me, ma'am!"

"You heard me correctly! My man was fucking one of your maids. I don't know her name, but I'm sure you can check your records to locate the bitch who was assigned to clean my room. I want this man out of my room. Please send up security to remove him, before I cut off his balls!" Shay said in a calm, but serious tone.

"Ma'am—"

Shay dropped the phone on the cradle, cutting off the man's response. She turned to find Michael had put on his briefs.

"I want you out of here!"

"Shay, please..."

"If you want to risk our relationship on that wanton woman, you can sleep with *her* for the remainder of the trip! There is no way you're *ever* touching this again," she said, pointing to her pussy.

§

Hours later, after all the madness with the hotel manager and security, Michael and his things were finally escorted out of the hotel. Shay was disillusioned by love. She gazed out of the resort's window and stared at the tranquility of the ocean as the memories of her very first visit to the island and to the Almond Morgan Bay Beach Resort as it ran through her mind. She and her two cousins, Nia and Tatiana, took a seven-day Caribbean cruise aboard a luxury ship. They flew into San Juan, Puerto Rico, and for six days, the ship docked at a different port. The last stop was the *best* of the entire cruise. They were only on the island of St. Lucia for eight hours; so for two hours, they shopped for souvenirs for their family and friends. The remaining time they wanted to hit the beach. Someone from town recommended that resort, and a group of them from the ship piled into two taxi vans to take them there. They even arranged a pickup. In four hours, they were on their way back to the ship.

The Almond Morgan Bay Beach Resort was small, but impressive, nevertheless. It sat right *on* the beach. Shay tipped across the marble floor because she didn't want to scratch it with the heels on her sandals. In awe, she stopped in front of the marble front desk, mesmerized by the largest fish tank she'd ever seen mounted on the wall. Exotic fish, her favorite bicolor Angelfish, Butterfly fish, and Cinnamon Clownfish swam around the tank, each fighting for tiny bites of food. She had always wanted to invest in a saltwater fish tank, but found in her research that it was expensive and time-consuming. Shay was fascinated watching the fish, until Tatiana dragged her into the restroom to change into their bathing suits. They then followed the path that led straight down to the beach, acting like they were paying guests at the resort.

Her first impression of the beach and the ocean was that they were breathtaking—reminding her of a panoramic scene on a postcard. The turquoise ocean looked delicious and inviting. The sand was fine and reminded her of powdered sugar. It was hot to her feet and free of debris, unlike the beaches in Philly.

This is paradise! Shay kept telling herself.

Shay ran into the ocean and played like she was a five-year-old child. The water was warm and soothing against her skin. She lost herself in it, diving and following the exotic fish. Three hours later, Nia and Tatiana literally dragged Shay out of the water because the cruise ship was leaving the port in two hours.

Time had moved much too quickly for Shay.

She cried in the restroom. Grudgingly, she towel dried her body, and slipped back into her clothes. Her heart was heavy; she had fallen in love with the island of St. Lucia, and promised herself she would return. Her next trip to the island of St. Lucia would be on an airplane, and she'd check into the Almond Morgan Bay Beach Resort for at least seven days.

This was *that* vacation.

Three years later, Shay and her boyfriend, Michael, checked into the Almond Morgan Bay Beach Resort. They hit The Pulse Club the evening of their arrival, and that was her first chance to check out the beach. While she was sunning, Michael was fucking that tramp.

The knock on the door brought Shay out of her musings.

"Shay, come on, Boo. You know that woman didn't mean anything to me!" Michael hollered from outside of her door. "It's been you and me these past three years," he whined.

"I'm supposed to forgive your infidelity and insensitivity to my feelings?"

"Shay, she crawled into the bed. Kissed and licked my back. I turned onto my back and she took my dick into her mouth. I thought she was you, Boo!"

"She looks nothing like me, Michael!" This proved how trifling he really was.

"I know. I know. But, I was too far gone to stop her."

"I don't need a stroke-by-stroke description. If you don't get away from my door I'll call security and have you permanently banned from this hotel!"

"I'm leaving, but this isn't over, Shay. I'll give you some time to calm down."

"Time won't fix this. It's over, Michael! I'm done! Go back to your trick!" Shay yelled back.

Nia and Tatiana had wanted her to dump Michael years ago. This was an eye-opening experience that left Shay reeling. She was finished with Michael. From then on, she would control her own destiny.

§

Shay wanted sex—meaningless, hot torrential sex!

That night, she returned to The Pulse Club without Michael—dressed scandalously, in a red mini dress that screamed that she was hunting for a *sexual* escapade. There was very little fabric covering her caramel flesh. The sleeveless dress outlined her firm breasts and cut dangerously across her flat abdomen. It scooped low down her back, and hugged all of her feminine curves. It was supposed to be a surprise for Michael; but now, she wasn't going to allow him to spoil the rest of her vacation. She used the dress for another purpose: as a seduction tool.

An hour later, three business suit-clad men sauntered into the club while she was planted at the bar, guzzling her third glass of Rum Punch. A dark-haired, violet-eyed gent sat across from her. Even from where Shay sat, she saw the color of his eyes was hypnotizing.

He carried himself with a commanding air of self-confidence, and she wanted a taste of him.

§

Linden David Stewart, CEO of Stewart International, along with two of his employees, entered The Pulse Club to unwind with a drink. He'd just signed the biggest deal for the company since his father stepped down as CEO over fourteen months ago. Linden had worked his butt off, proving to his dad that he hadn't made a mistake choosing him to run the family's business. His father, David Stewart Sr., retired to spend more time with his wife. However, he remained as chairman of the board, and Linden's boss.

Linden spotted the caramel beauty seated at the bar the moment he entered the club. That part of his body came to life when he brushed past her on his way to their table.

What is the name of that scent she's wearing? he silently asked himself.

It had a fruity scent. Blackberry came to his mind—sweet, scrumptious, and sensuous—like the woman seated at the bar. Linden wanted an even closer view of her curvaceous body. He wanted to ride her until she hollered his name, and he released his seed in her succulent core.

"Linden, do you want your usual?" Thurston Taylor Chandler Jr. asked him for the second time. Everyone called him by his last name, Chandler.

He snapped out of his musing and ordered a double Scotch. The auburn-haired waitress standing over Linden was dressed in a skimpy top exposing 40 DD breasts. Her short skirt stopped at the crack of her plump ass. She smiled seductively down at Linden.

He didn't notice the waitress, because his eyes were still fastened on the woman seated at the bar. She captivated him.

Trina, the waitress shook her hips as she strutted away, knowing that her ample figure was tempting the men at the table.

Chandler's intense, blue eyes followed the exotic Caribbean waitress, who wore hardly any clothes.

"Give me one Scotch, no water, and two Coronas," Trina said to the bartender. She turned back to stare at their table. The violet-eyed gent interested Trina.

"Linden, you seem miles away. Are you all right?" inquired Chandler.

"I just need to unwind from our meeting with the Prime Minister," Linden said to Chandler, the vice president of sales, who was also his best friend since the sixth grade.

Peter Andrew, his assistant said, "what you need boss is to get laid!"

"Yes, I'm in agreement!" Chandler chimed in. His eyes scanned the club to scope out the offerings. "There are plenty of beauties here tonight."

Linden laughed at their suggestion. That certain part of his body hardened at the mention of feeling a woman's soft hands, other than his own kneading and stroking his erection until it burst. He hadn't been laid in over a year. Not since he began his reign at Stewart International. All of his concentration has been on bringing in new clients for the business, reducing expenses, and making a profit.

§

The calypso music was pumping. Steel brass drums played Shay's song, and she boldly danced over to their table. Using her hips, she bumped the dark haired man against the shoulder.

Linden's eyes slid over her clinging red dress—stopping at the center of her femininity. His gaze slid down her caramel thighs and back up to her shimmering hazel eyes.

"Dance with me," Shay commanded. The look of unbridled lust filled her eyes.

Motioning with her hips, Shay extended her arms out, inviting him to follow her. He didn't hesitate. Awestruck by her antics, he eased out of his chair with his long, lean legs, and followed her onto the dance floor.

"Go get her, Linden. Taste some of that caramel delight," Chandler and Peter urged.

Shay wasn't offended by his friend's words; after all, she had changed her game plan. She'd never tried *vanilla* and tonight *anything* was game!

The rum punch had already warmed Shay's insides, loosened her inhibited soul, and she created *quite* a show as she rocked and swayed to the Caribbean beat. Her booty gyrated against the ever-growing tent in Linden's pants.

The music *finally* slowed to allow them to hold one another, and his fingers slid sensuously over her bare arms—pulling her snug against his body.

Linden exuded masculinity, a hard, muscular chest, and tight abs. He had *everything* Shay wanted in a man. Their hands intertwined, and their bodies fit perfectly—causing friction toward the center of their sex.

Shay gazed into his eyes. His sparkling violet eyes were clear one minute and smoldering the next.

"What is the name of the perfume you're wearing?" he asked in a deep and sensual southern drawl, sending a ripple of awareness through her.

"I'm wearing Blackberry cologne. Do you like?"

"Yes, I do," Linden said, his nose sliding closer for a deeper sniff.

"I like your scent, too. As a matter of fact I want to *taste* you," she said in a silky-velvety voice that ran all over him like melted butter.

"Oh God…what are you doing to me?" he murmured into her ear.

"What am *I* doing to *you?*" Shay cooed back into his ear, blew against his neck, and licked his pulse point—now throbbing from his excitement.

"We're being *watched*."

"Let them watch." She trailed kisses from her hot, ripened lips up his smooth neck.

"You're so *hot!*"

"And *you're* so *ready.*"

Shay's hands slid between them and stroked his ever-growing member.

"Come-to-my-suite," he groaned, stumbling over his words, as she suddenly grabbed his jewel, and gently squeezed it.

"I'll meet you outside," she purred into his ear and gave him another squeeze.

Reluctantly, Linden released her. He took deep, long breaths to calm himself, as he walked back to his table. He pulled out his wallet and tossed a hundred dollar bill on the table.

"I'm out of here!" he announced, his smile had a spark of eroticism.

He picked up his Scotch and chugged it down. It slid down and burned his throat and tears glistened in his unusual violet-colored eyes. "Chandler, tomorrow morning if I'm not at the airport, you and Peter take the company's plane and go on home without me. If she's as good as she looks, I'll be taking a well-deserved vacation."

"Enjoy!" Chandler said, grinning from ear to ear.

"Yes, hump that piece of meat until she can't walk, boss," Peter said crudely.

"Show some respect, man! The boss doesn't use women that way, unlike you who'll stick his rod between any woman's thighs." Chandler chuckled, a nasty tone in his voice.

Linden shook his head in disgust. If Peter wasn't a damn good assistant he would've gotten rid of him a long time again. He swept past women and men dancing and gyrating with their partners on his way toward the entrance of the club. It had been over a year since he had sex. Tonight, he was going to make up for that and more!

§

Michael and his island slut were standing at the entrance to the club. He couldn't believe *his* Shay had created quite a show—and with a *white* man. She was all over him, and he was jealous as hell.

Shay tried to walk past him; his fierce grip on her arms stopped her in mid-motion.

"What are you doing, Shay?"

"I'm *slumming*, just like you," she returned. "But then again, he doesn't look like a bum, and I'll bet he has more money than you!"

"But he's *white!*"

"And he has the same equipment as you—maybe even *bigger*," she retorted.

Smiling sweetly, Shay stepped out of his path and continued on her quest.

"Do you *know* that man?" Linden asked when he caught up to her.

"That was *nobody*," she declared, quickly taking his hand and they walked out of the club.

"I don't *like* to share!" He stated firmly, his unusual, violet eyes looking right through her.

"I'm not into sharing, either!" she returned, staring back at him. Her eyes didn't waver from his fierce grip.

"This is your last chance to walk away."

"I *want* you!"
"What is your name?"

He didn't know the name of the caramel beauty he invited back to his suite.

"I'm Shay Bennett."

"And I'm Linden David Stewart. You're something else, Ms. Bennett," he said, kissing the seam of her lips. "I can't wait to dissolve within that *hot* body of yours."

Shay's eyes skimmed down the length of Linden's pants; his cock seemed to expand before her eyes.

"I'm ready for you to show me what you got, *white* boy."

"Oh, I can deliver," he whispered into her ear.

With a wicked grin on his face, he nudged her into the first cab that pulled to the curb, and told the driver to drop them at the Jade Mountain Resort.

Chapter Two

Moist lips kissed the cheeks of her buttocks, and followed a path up the middle of her back, her shoulders, neck, and finally her earlobes.

Shay awakened from the most pleasurable sleep she had in months, until the added enticement of Linden's morning erection thumped against her ass.

"Mmm," she moaned from the heat of his kisses. She turned onto her back, and his lips—demandingly hot and hungry, descended upon hers.

She moaned from the persistence of his tongue lapping at her closed lips until she smiled. Her lips opened for him.

Linden's tongue swept through the opening of her mouth like a lethal weapon. His tongue sent shivers of desire racing through her. Heat radiated straight down to her quivering core.

Hot. Wet. Pulsating.

His tongue was in her mouth and his passion—thickens, insisting, at the apex of her purring haven.

Shay's legs spread apart instinctively to receive more. The head of his erection thumped insistently against her moist center.

"Ahh...Michael, that's it, babe. Right there—"

"Michael! Who the *hell* is Michael?"

Her eyes opened, blinked, and refocused on the most dazzling pair of violet eyes she had *ever* seen.

Shay's eyes widened in surprise.

He was *white—hot-deliciously-handsome*, and *not* Michael.

He had a cleft chin, sensual lips, and the brightest smile any woman would've wanted to wake up next to. Ink-colored, blue-black hair graced his head. It tapered on the top, but was longer down his neck. He had hair across his chest and his muscular arms, ending at his belly button.

He lifted her body, and lowered her slowly onto his rock-hard erection—which was now deeply embedded between her thighs. The contrast in their skin tones—vanilla next to caramel—was quite delicious, as if she had been eating ice cream. Suddenly, he slid out of her with just the head of his shaft kissing her dewy core.

"L-Linden?"

"Yes, I'm glad to hear you remember who I am. Now, who is Michael?"

"Ahh...Michael...was my *past*," she said quickly.

"I remind you of him?"

"No! You most certainly *do* not," Shay moaned, from the fierce heat of him. Her body shuddered and hummed.

The smile in his eyes contained a sensuous flame. He glided back into her; and intensely, she matched his sensual rhythm—beat for beat, until she exploded. Breathless, she lay under him as he climaxed feverishly. His love was hot and oozed between their bodies, filling her walls.

Shay's eyes popped open, again, and registered the fact that his seed saturated between them. She was *not* using any birth control. She thought about how Michael always used a condom. *Damn, that third glass of rum punch. What the hell am I thinking, picking up this man last night?* she thought.

The sex was mind-boggling-hot, earth-shattering-fierce and he was hung like a brother. That was of no consequence, because she wasn't looking to start a family just yet.

"Linden, let me up. What are you doing?"

Shay pounded on Linden's muscular back trying to move an unmovable body, and to stop the oozing of his fluid.

"What is it?" He snapped. She couldn't miss the irritation in his voice.

"Get off me!" she cried out.

Spent, Linden pulled out of Shay's body before collapsing face down on top of the pillow.

Shay leaped out of bed and dashed into the bathroom, washing Linden's semen from between her legs. She attempted to blot away as much as she could. Angry, she ran back into the bedroom where he was still lying on his stomach.

"Linden, wake up!" She yelled, and hit him on his back.

"Shay, you're wearing me out, woman! I need some sleep," he mumbled.

"Where's the condom?"

"What?"

He rolled onto his back, and his beautiful eyes stared back at her. A confused look crossed his face.

"You didn't use a condom, Linden!" she accused.

"Aren't you using some means of protection?"

"Hell no, I'm not. Damn you! You may have AIDS or impregnated me!" Shay screamed.

"First of all, Ms. Shay Bennett, I've been tested, and I do *not* have AIDS. Secondly, I've been celibate for over a year, and that accounts for me thinking with the wrong head last night. *You* came onto *me;* and if you play the game, you should be able to deal with the consequences!"

"What the hell does *that* mean?"

"Come back to bed. I don't want to fight about this."

"Why, so you can plant more of your seed inside of me? No, thank you!"

Linden burst out laughing. His infectious laugh was like warm honey coating her heated flesh. With his back pressed against the wood headboard he sat up. His erect member stood at attention once again.

"Are you on some kind of male enhancement drugs?"

"This is *all* me, sweetheart. I've been celibate, remember?"

Shay's eyes traveled the length of his body, flashed back, and she tingled all over. She remembered every thrust, every moan, and cry of pleasure she'd received in his arms. Michael couldn't *touch* him as a lover. Linden was as smooth as silk, and her body was still humming from their last go-round.

"Shay, I've been inside of your beautiful body at least *three* times since early this morning. It's a little *late* to worry about that, now!"

"You're *not* touching me again *without* a condom, Linden!" She exclaimed, backing away from the bed.

"But you know you want it," he said, getting on his knees. He lunged for her hands.

The ringing of his cell phone distracted Linden. Shay took that opportunity to slip out of his clutches over to the other side of the suite—where she planted her naked body on the chaise.

Linden's long fingers snatched up the cell phone off the nightstand.

"Hi Mom," the tone of his voice became even warmer, like liquid butter.

Why am I still there? Shay thought.

This was the *perfect* opportunity for Shay to pick up her dress and leave, but she *wanted* to stay. He still had a hold on her, or more like his body held her captive. It was as if an invisible force kept her inside of his suite. She barely knew the man. Intimately, she knew every one of his erotic zones, but she wanted *more*. Shay wanted to know all there was to know about Mr. Linden David Stewart—the man.

He stood naked—perfectly comfortable—talking to his mother. Shay's ears perked up when she heard him mention he'd met a woman in St. Lucia.

"Yes, I know it's unusual for me to extend my trip. The others flew home this morning, but I thought I'd take a well-deserved vacation, Mom."

He stared at Shay. His eyes sparkled like parts of the Caribbean Ocean.

"Maybe," he said. He boldly stroked himself as he watched her.

What is he doing? Shay wondered and said to herself.

Her feminine walls started to throb, as if he were telepathically sending out his desires—filling her, pleasuring her. She wanted him again.

"Mom, I'll call you later. My cell phone is down to one bar. It needs to be charged," he lied with smoothness and style.

Linden was off the cell phone in a flash.

"Hey, what are you doing?"

Shay backed against the chaise. Linden's smoldering eyes scared her in an exciting and tantalizing way. Her arousal dripped down her thighs.

"I need to be recharged, Shay."

"No!"

"I'm taking what's mine," he groaned.

The amber flames in her eyes and her dazzling smile aroused him even more.

"Oh, yeah?" she cooed, totally breathless.

Her coo was like a feather tickling his eardrums, and Linden became even more turned on. In fact, he'd never been that hard and he never wanted a woman more.

"I most certainly plan to," he said, smiling down at her.

His smile has a spark of eroticism, but I can't resist, Shay thought.

Linden swept her into his arms, and carried her back to bed, gently laying her down.

Their eyes locked and held, smoldering embers in them.

Shay licked her dry lips with anticipation.

Linden got down on his knees. With just the tip of his thumb, he sent a ripple of desire through her as he

~ 20 ~

trailed his thumb down her belly, to the lips of her femininity, and gently pulled back the dewy, soft petals.

"Linden?"

His head slid lower.

He caressed her body with his tongue, at first, and then he went in for the kill. Relentlessly, his tongue darted in and out of her quivering mound. Her nipples hardened and the blackberry hues puckered from desire.

"Ahh...Linden," she cried out, as the heat inside of her body coiled. Molten shafts of sensation rippled down her body to her quaking center.

He held Shay down with her legs spread apart while he lapped up the essence of her passion.

"L-i-n-d-e-n!" She cried out his name in a frenzied delight.

Shay was going insane with desire. Fire radiated throughout her body. Automatically, her hips writhed against the mattress, and her head flopped back and forth, as she surrendered herself to the heat of Linden's tongue. Her fingers threaded through his hair as she gyrated her hips, and rammed his head deeper into her moist-throbbing-folds.

"I'm-I'm...cumming!" Shay cried out after her first orgasm rippled into the next. Seconds seemed to go on forever. Her thighs, calves, and ankles quivered, uncontrollably as if she were having a seizure. Time stood still. Her body felt buoyant and her fingers felt weightless when they slid out of his hair. Her breaths were ragged and she surrendered to the spasms.

Minutes later, Linden's tongue eased out of her pulsating haven, and he nudged the head of his shaft between her moist thighs.

Shay wanted to protest, but his thrusts were slow and measured as he hit every one of her sensitive spots.

She *couldn't* protest and her willpower slipped away. Instead, she arched her hips to meet his thrusts, over and over again, until her third orgasm more powerful than the last, left her crying out in euphoria. She had never felt so detached, yet connected to *another* soul.

§

That evening, he found a store that provided him with enough condoms for them to use for a full week. Linden was *insatiable,* and he took Shay's body in every conceivable way. She loved it!

Shay returned to Almond Morgan Bay Beach Resort to pack up her things. She wouldn't need two rooms. Linden's suite was *much* more elegant, and it included him as an added bonus!

Her eyes scanned Linden's luxury suite. It was obvious he wasn't hurting for money. The Star Infinity Pool Suite had to cost him a pretty penny. The Jade Mountain Resort was St Lucia's newest and exclusive resort, she had read. And it sat on top of the mountain.

The bedroom was spacious: two of Shay's studio apartments back home in the Philly's University City, could fit into that room. His suite included a 450 square feet private infinity pool. It was on the other side of the living room, and it replaced the fourth wall. When they swam toward the edge of the pool, they could see the beauty of the Pitons Mountains, and gazed down at the shimmering turquoise Caribbean Sea. The architectural design of the resort was unbelievable, and the missing fourth wall allowed them to feel the cool breeze off the ocean.

This suite is an aphrodisiac for romance – seduction in its own right – with no television or telephone to distract a couple from one another. It's private sanctuary and perfect for a couple on their honeymoon, she thought.

§

After their marathon rounds of making love, Shay lay her head against Linden's chest. He told her about his taking over as CEO a year ago, and the big shoes he had to fill—his father and his grandfather's. Shay shared the details of her parents' deaths; they died in an automobile accident when she was sixteen years old. She went to live with her mother's sister, Aunt Lilly, until she moved out four years ago. She was attending night school and working toward her Bachelor's degree in accounting. They were both only children. Linden was lonely growing up except for his best friend, Chandler, and Shay had her cousins: Nia, Taj and Tatiana, to keep her company. They talked until satiety lulled their bodies to sleep.

Chapter Three

For three glorious days, their moonlight swims led to making love under the stars and falling asleep in each other's arms. They woke up to a new day as Mother Nature's showers bathed their naked entwined bodies.

There was no need for them to depart from Linden's suite. The resort's amenities catered to their every desire. The food was scrumptious and was delivered to them by their personal staff. It fueled their bodies for the next several rounds, until their sexual appetite for one another was appeased.

When they finally came up for air, Linden wanted to explore the island of St. Lucia. The adventurous side of him urged Shay to go mountain climbing with him. He showered and dressed leaving the suite to make the arrangements at the resort's concierge desk.

Shay just wanted to stay walled up in the king-sized bed.

Why is the bed always much more comfortable when you check into a hotel? She thought.

There was Egyptian cotton bedding and a Memory Foam mattress that contoured to her body, and eased the ache in her lower back. Shay cuddled under the blanket and drifted back to sleep. She had no intentions of ever leaving that bed.

§

Two hours later, Linden swept through the suite. He entered the bedroom loaded down with shopping bags in both hands. He removed: boots and denim shorts for him, and black biker's shorts for her, T-shirts, and all the equipment they would need for the climb, dumping his purchases on top of the bed.

Startled, Shay stretched out her arms and knocked the two pairs of boots off the bed.

"What's all of this?" She asked in a deep husky tone.

"I've purchased everything we'd need for mountain climbing, sweetheart."

"You're crazy if you think I'm going to climb some God-forsaken mountain, Linden!"

"It's not a God-forsaken mountain, it's the Petit Piton Mountain, Shay. It's the smallest mountain on St Lucia."

"No! I'm staying right here in this bed," she said adamantly kicking the rest of his purchases onto the floor. She pulled the blanket back over her chilled, naked, flesh. "I don't need *any* more exercise. My body is already aching in places I've never been touched, Linden!"

"We're not going to climb to the top of the mountain, just to the waterfall. We can go swimming, and you can relieve some of that pent-up tension, Shay."

"I don't have any pent-up tension! We've been hitting it for *three* days—three days. All I want to do is take a hot, soothing bubble bath, maybe get a massage or possibly a swim in your pool."

"We'll do all of that tomorrow."

She groaned. "Why can't we do something less strenuous? Like sitting in a car and driving through the volcano, touring the island, or a dinner cruise along the Caribbean Sea? I'll even go along if you wanted to go scuba diving or snorkeling, but climbing a damn mountain—hell *no*, Linden!"

"Please, Shay...I've *always* wanted to climb that mountain. Two years ago, when I was last here, I promised myself if I should ever return. I would make time to climb it."

"*No!*"

"Just think how sexy you'll look in a pair of black biker shorts, and a slinky pink tank shirt. I brought one for you, and a pair of boots to cover those beautiful toes of yours," he murmured in her ear.

He planted kisses all over her oval-shaped face until their lips met and his hands cupped each of her breasts.

Shay trembled under his skillful fingers.

"Linden...no," she sighed.

"I say...yes, Shay!"

§

Shay found herself trailing up the Petit Piton Mountain following Linden's cute, tight buns every step of the way. She had to admit the scenery was breathtaking halfway up the mountain. But it was *hot* as hell. They managed to catch a cool breeze every once in a while. Beads of perspiration ran down her face, and the end of her ponytail stuck to her damp neck.

"Shay, move it, sweetheart. Denzel says we're almost to the middle of the mountain."

Denzel, an umber-colored brother with dreadlocks down to his hips, was their friendly guide. When he smiled, she couldn't miss his two gold front teeth and a deep dimple embedded in his right cheek. He met them outside of the resort in a yellow Jeep Wrangler. He seemed very knowledgeable and pointed out all of the tourist hot spots, as he drove them to the base of the mountain.

"I'm melting, Linden," she complained, stopping for a moment to wipe her forehead.

Why in the hell did I allow him to talk me into doing this? It was those damn mesmerizing eyes of his and those sensuous fingers of his trailing all over my body. Linden gets my motor running, and then he picked me up and tossed me in the shower. I needed a cold blast of waters hosing down my flesh, after the way he aroused my body.

"There's supposed to be a waterfall not far from here. We can strip and take a swim," he hollered down to her.

"I didn't bring a swimsuit, Linden."

"Sweetheart, you don't need a swimsuit," he said, in that sexy, southern drawl of his.

Oh my…it's happening again. My body's humming.

"You're crazy! What about Denzel? There might be others on this mountain?" she added.

"I'll take care of it; just keep climbing, Shay. It's just another couple of feet, and then you can cool off."

§

Minutes later, Linden extended his hands out to Shay to pull her over the last boulder.

The minute Shay stepped past that large boulder; she released his hands and looked down the side of the mountain to see how far she had climbed. That was a mistake. Her sunglasses fell to the ground, and she swayed, suddenly dizzy from the height. She grabbed Linden's elbow to steady herself.

Why didn't I tell him about my fear of heights?

"Sweetheart, are you all right?" Linden inquired.

He pulled her into his arms, and her ass bumped up against his erection.

"I just got dizzy for a moment," she said, ignoring the state of his arousal.

That man is always hard and ready, she thought.

"Ma'am, what yuh need is a drink of water," Denzel said, as he offered her a cold bottle of water from his Knapsack.

Denzel picked up her sunglasses and passed it to Linden.

Shay gulped down half the bottle of water in seconds. It relieved her parched throat, and then she leaned further into Linden's damp body, trembling suddenly.

"You're shaking, Shay. Are you sure you're all right?" Linden questioned. His hands caressed her damp arms.

"I'm fine," she mumbled, pushing out of his arms. She walked away from the ledge, taking deep breaths. "It's beautiful up here, and I wished I'd thought to bring my video camera."

Shay was still trembling, but happy she'd just conquered her fear of heights. Instead, she focused on the panoramic views of both the Petit and the Gros Pitons Mountains. Together, they looked like two cone-shaped peaks. The sky was crystal clear—not a cloud in sight, and she continued to take deep breaths needing this picturesque view to calm her trembling body.

"*Shay?*" Linden watched her closely.

"Do you have a camera, Linden?" Shay inquired.

She wanted to capture this moment. How could she have walked out of his suite without her video camera?

"No, I didn't bring one to St. Lucia," he said, looking at her flushed cheeks.

"Ma'am, yuh can buy postcards of the Petit Piton and the Gros Piton Mountains at the tourist station when we go back down the mountain. It's cheap."

"I'll do that. Thank you, Denzel," she said, giving him one of her brilliant smile.

Denzel returned her smile; bent his head, and then walked away as if he was shy being around a beautiful woman.

Linden saw the look of desire in Denzel's eyes. He watched the exchange between the two of them, and instantly became jealous. He pulled Shay back into his arms, and tightened his grip around her narrow waist.

She looked back at him, and the smile in his eyes contained that sensuous flame again.

"Denzel, how tall is this mountain?" Shay inquired, as she fought her desire to kiss Linden's lips.

"Ma'am, the Petit Piton is one of two mountains overlooking the Soufriére Bay. It's about 2461 feet," Denzel declared.

Shay couldn't miss the enthusiasm and the pride in Denzel's voice when he spoke of *his* island.

Denzel bent down to pick up a leaf.

"This is the leaf of life," he told her.

Shay left the confines of Linden's arms to take the leaf Denzel extended to her.

It appeared to be just an ordinary green leaf. She turned it over and saw nothing unusual about it.

"When yuh break a piece of that leaf, it will grow back. See, these roots will allow it to regenerate," he said, once again with pride. "It can also be used as medicine to cure the common cold."

"How is that feasible?" Linden walked over to Shay, and he took the leaf out of her hands.

"We boil it in a pot of water, add a little sugar, and yuh drink it for about three days. It can also be applied to the skin to treat fungus."

Shay took the leaf back from Linden.

"Now, I see why you call it 'The Leaf of life,' Denzel. I wish I could bring it back to Philly," Shay added.

She believed in using herbs and home remedies to cure her ailments, instead of prescribed medication.

"Sorry, ma'am, yuh can't bring home."

"I know I can't, Denzel," Shay said, smiling at him. "One can only wish."

Linden watched the exchange inpatient to be alone with Shay. He was so hard he would explode any minute if he didn't feel her vaginal walls clenching him sweetly. The present conversation between Shay and Denzel bored him.

"Where's that waterfall, Denzel? We'd like to take a dip," Linden replied curtly.

"Not far, come, Mr. Stewart."

Shay smacked Linden on the ass the moment Denzel turned his back.

He gave her a smile that sent her pulse racing.

She knew what he wanted. Being with Linden for the past three days reminded her that his sexual appetite was unquenchable. He took her right hand and pulled her along the rocky trail, eager to get to the waterfall.

Shay admitted to herself that she wanted a dip in the waterfall, too.

§

The sounds of cascading water played soothing tones as they approached the waterfall.

Denzel extended his hands out to them. "This is the Piton Waterfall."

Shay was awestruck by the view before her. There were three separate streams flowing into one waterfall. Surrounding them was a collection of foliages—including banana trees and coconut palms trees. The temperature seemed to drop about twenty degrees, there. It was cooler now. The water was inviting, and the winding stone path leading down to the waterfall beckoned her to come a little closer.

It's breathtakingly primitive and tranquil. Whoever constructed this little piece of heaven, must have been a romantic at heart, Shay thought.

"The waterfall rises about 30 feet in the air," Denzel said, stepping closer to her.

"It's breathtaking," Shay said softly, her eyes glazing over in wonder.

"The temperature of the water varies from lukewarm to hot, and the water is known to heal the body. A swim in that water will leave your body refreshed and relaxed," he added.

Shay longed for a dip. Her thong was sticking in the crack of her ass, and the biker shorts now stuck to her thighs as if it were permanently glued to her body. She gazed at Linden, smiling suggestively for him to make it happen.

"Denzel, we'd like to take a private dip," Linden stated in his commanding voice.

He pulled out five crisp one hundred dollar bills out of the pocket of his T-shirt and handed it to him. "We just need an hour. Do *whatever* you need to do to keep *everyone* away from the waterfall. I'd like a little alone time with *my* woman."

Denzel's eyes lit up when Mr. Stewart dropped the crisp bills into his hands. All he had to do was to keep everyone away from the waterfall. He *could* do that.

"Yes, Mr. Stewart," he said, tucking the bills in his back pocket, walking back down the trail.

"You're *so* sneaky, Mr. Stewart," Shay cooed.

"I want you, *now!*" he said, and his southern accent was thick from desire.

Linden pinned her with a long, silent scrutiny.

The air crackled around them.

He didn't have to touch her, yet the memories of them coming together physically—automatically replayed in her head.

Shay felt the tips of Linden's fingers follow the curves of her breasts. His hot breath fanned her right cheek. The smell of butterscotch candy, which he had just sucked, wafted under her nostrils. The water bouncing against the rocks cooed to the horny lovers.

She gazed into his shimmering eyes. The fierce heat of him against her caused her to melt fast. Time stood still when she felt Linden slide off her biker shorts and thong at the same time, then her damp tank shirt. It was only hours ago when they last made love, he proceeded to take her yet again right beside the waterfall.

Spellbound, with a single stroke of his thumb, he created a fire within her loins. His kisses were like a slow, moving drug, consuming Shay's breath. Keenly, she grasped for more of his intoxicating butterscotch kisses, until his tongue darted in and out of her pulsating, dewy clit. His lips devoured her heat, his tongue sopped up every morsel, and she sighed from the sweet torrent of pleasure washing over her body.

Seconds later, Shay couldn't take it any longer. She needed *all* of him. Her fingers struggled to release his sex. Trembling, she fought to unbuckle his pants, and broke the nail on her right thumb. Her desires for him were primitive… electrifying. She took a deep breath to calm herself, wanting this feeling to last forever. At last, she was able to knead his heated flesh, and she moaned with expectation.

His flesh was hot, velvety smooth. His manhood was hard, long and thick when she stroked it from the head to the base.

Linden groaned.

Seconds later, Linden lifted her body and thrusted between her silken thighs, repeatedly, entering her succulent core. His heavy erection kissed, planted, and settled within her quivering, moist heat.

Shay surrendered under his skillful hands. She convulsed, her body clenched him, and she melted as Linden's release exploded within her. His hot semen flooded her vaginal walls without restraint. Consumed by a blazing ecstasy, they slid under the waterfall as it cooled their already sated bodies.

Underneath the St. Lucia's Piton waterfall, Shay stood captivated by the water rushing down their enmeshed bodies.

§

Later, hand in hand, the lovers walked out of the waterfall, and into the hot stream where the water enfolded them, and soaked their sated flesh. They swam and played like two kids until Linden dragged Shay over to the rocks and to their discarded clothes. The sun was so hot; it dried their bodies, instantaneously. Reluctantly, they redressed and waited for Denzel to lead them back down the mountain.

Shay held Linden's hands and gazed around at the romantic paradise they had found. This was one day of her vacation she would never forget. She was falling in love for the very *first* time in her life.

Ten minutes later, there was a tinge of sadness in her eyes, as Shay climbed the path back down the mountain.

Chapter Four

Shay and Linden overslept the next day. After climbing the Petit Piton Mountain, making love in the waterfall, the dip in the hot stream left their bodies refreshed. They climbed back down the mountain, and returned to their resort feeling lethargic. Linden ordered room service; they ate in bed, and ended up making love again.

It was after one o'clock before they crawled out of bed. Their bodies ached from yesterday's workout, and both of them were moving a little slower this afternoon.

"What would you like to eat?" Linden asked.

He pulled out the room service menu, scanning the breakfast and lunch selections.

"I'm starving. Please order me whatever you're having," she hollered, easing into the whirlpool tub. She needed to soak her aching limbs. It was large enough to accommodate both of them. She had hoped Linden would join her, but he seemed more interested in food right then.

Linden picked up the phone to dial room service. He ordered a pitcher of champagne mimosa, baked saltfish, two steaks, scrambled eggs, bacon, dumplings, and a fruit medley of sliced mangos, bananas, and green figs. He was famished, and there was enough food to feed a party of four.

He removed his cell phone out of his briefcase and pressed the speed dial to call his parents' home. The phone rang four times, and he was about to end the call when his father's booming voice spoke into his ear.

"Dad," Linden said into the phone. He walked out of the bedroom into the living room because he wanted a little privacy.

"Son, I read the contracts, and you couldn't have negotiated a better deal for the company. I'm so proud of you!"

"Thank you, Dad. I worked really hard on that deal."

"It shows. I was surprised when your mother mentioned that you decided to stay on in St. Lucia. Are you enjoying your vacation?" he asked.

"I didn't realize how much I needed a break until I landed on the island."

"It's been fourteen months since you took over the day-to-day operation of running Stewart International. You deserve some down time, son."

"I climbed the Petit Piton Mountain, yesterday," he stated with pride.

"Be careful, son. I don't want anything to happen to my *only* son. And, I won't tell your mother what you've been up to."

"Please, don't tell her. She'll just worry."

"Tell me you won't be climbing that second mountain."

Linden burst out laughing. "No, Dad, I've done all the mountain climbing I plan to do this trip."

"Great! When can we expect you back in Maryland?"

"I'm returning on Saturday."

"Your mother and I expect you in Virginia for Sunday dinner."

"I'll be there," he said, pacing the living room. Shay was on his mind as well as the developing feeling he could *no* longer deny.

"Dad, when you met Mom, how long before you knew you were in love with her?"

"I fell in love with your mother the moment I gazed into her doe brown eyes and when she refused to go out on a date with me. I knew I *had* to have her. She was a challenge. It took only two months to capture her."

"Dad?"

"You've met a woman?"

He smiled at how attuned his father was to their conversation.

"Linden will you wash my back?" Shay hollered from the bathroom.

His eyes turned to the bedroom.

"She's with you, now?" his father asked, hearing her called out to his son.

"I have to go, Dad."

"You have to tell me *something*; otherwise your mother will blow up your cell phone, son."

"I've met a woman..."

The knock on the suite's door stopped him from saying more.

"Linden, I need you!" Shay hollered, again.

"Dad, I'll talk to you when I get home."

Linden closed his cell phone, while opening the door to his suite.

"Mr. Stewart, I have your room service." Reggie said, smiling at the white man who tipped generously.

"Reggie, how are you man?" Linden politely asked as he shook his hand. Linden charmed everyone he met, including the staff at the resort.

"I'm doing well, and I have that package you requested."

Reggie slipped a small white envelope into his hand.

"Thanks man! She's going to love this," he said, tucking the envelope into the pocket of his robe.

"Where would you like me to set up, sir?" Reggie politely asked.

"The usual location will be okay," Linden said.

Reggie, a tall, mahogany-colored young man wheeled in the rolling cart containing their meal into the suite. He was one of the kitchen staff, and Linden met him the very first day of his stay. Swiftly and efficiently, he set up the dining table besides the pool. He lit the candle centerpiece and put the final touch on the table when from the corner of his eyes, he glimpsed a caramel beauty.

Shay sauntered out of the bedroom with her hair piled on top of her head, dripping wet. Her bathrobe was wide open.

~ 38 ~

"Didn't you hear me calling you?" She whined. "I wanted you to wash my back."

Reggie's mouth dropped open. His hazel eyes shimmered with surprise at the woman in his sight. These last couple of days she was hidden in Mr. Stewart's bedroom whenever he delivered their meals. When she spotted him watching her, she quickly belted her robe. But not before he saw all of her goodies: her wet, caramel satiny skin, her firm breasts, her dark chocolate areolas, and her bare mound. He wanted to cock her, but she was obviously interested in only white men, he convinced himself.

"And our brunch is here. Come, let's go eat by the pool," Linden said, extending his hands for her to follow him.

"Shay, I'd like you to meet Reggie. He has been delivering our meals for the last couple of days," Linden said, as he boldly scribbled his signature on the bill.

"Ma'am," Reggie politely replied, but his eyes boldly raked across her body again.

Shay didn't like the look in his eyes, so she just nodded her head.

"Enjoy your meal, ma'am, sir," Reggie said, taking the receipt and the crisp bills from Linden's hands. He took another look at the beauty before walking through the doors.

Shay watched the door close behind Reggie.

"I called out to you twice, Linden. I wanted you to wash my back."

"Sweetheart, let's dine first, then we'll both take a bath."

Linden pulled out her chair.

~ 39 ~

Shay sat and he slid her closer to the table. Her eyes gazed across the glass table noticing there was enough food to feed an army of people.

He removed the lids off each dish.

"This looks and smells mouth-watering delicious, babe."

"Come on, dig in," he encouraged.

Shay loaded her plate and sampled saltfish, steak, dumplings, and the fruit. She ate every drop on her plate, and washed it down with two glasses of champagne mimosa.

"You've eaten quite a bit off that plate," he teased.

"*Me!* You can throw down as well, Linden."

"It must be all that fresh air and *exercise* I've been receiving, lately." He chuckled.

Shay unfastened her robe. She was ready to burst, and began to stroke her full stomach, while smiling back at Linden.

"Come here," he groaned, extending out his hand to her.

He removed their robes and eased their naked bodies down onto the large, black micro fiber chaise.

"I thought we were going to bathe together," Shay cooed, her eyes skimming over his body.

This is just as nice," he mumbled, nibbling on her neck. His thumb tweaked the tips of her right nipple. "You're wearing my favorite cologne again—Blackberry. I could eat you right now, Shay."

"The blacker the berry, the sweeter the juice," she whispered seductively. Her tongue swiped his ear, nipped, and then swiped it again.

"You're not black in coloring. You're more like caramel in coloring—together we're vanilla ice cream with caramel topping and a cherry on top," he stated.

Her tongue was setting him on fire again.

"Cherry—my cherry was busted a long time ago."

"I wished I'd been your first," Linden crooned, his left hand caressed her silken belly.

"My first time, I don't know what he was doing to me. There was no foreplay. He just stuck his *thing* into me, grunted and grinned because it was good to him. But for me, I couldn't wait for him to get *it* out of me."

"I'm sorry...your first time wasn't earth-shattering and invigorating," he whispered. Unconsciously, his fingers threaded through her hair until it tumbled carelessly down her shoulders. She looked uninhibited—downright sexy to his eyes.

"I felt nothing with him, and I've had several lovers since then."

"You're a passionate, giving lover, Shay," he said, nibbling on her chin.

"Ahh...with you, Linden, it's as if, I'm making love for the very first time. It feels so good—so right. I've never felt as connected as I do with you."

Their eyes locked.

She kissed his cleft chin.

"Shay...I..."

"No, you don't have to return my feelings."

Shay covered Linden's lips with her right hand.

"I just wanted to share that with you, and after drinking two glasses of champagne mimosas, it has given me loose lips."

"I care...Shay!"

She brushed her lips gently against his, and her arms curled around his waist automatically tightening.

"I like this, us just lounging around and talking like this, Shay."

"This feels good—natural," she said yawning into his chest.

Shay's eyes felt heavy, her stomach was full, and the heat from Linden's body made her aroused, but sleepy.

He didn't get a chance to tell her how they would be spending their evening that night.

"Shay, I managed to get tickets for the Jazz festival, tonight," Linden said into her hair.

Her eyes popped open.

"What did you say, babe?"

"I've got tickets for us to go to the festival, tonight, Shay," he enunciated each word slowly.

She bolted out of his arms.

"Are you *serious,* Linden?"

"Yes!" He sat up and reached for his robe and removed the envelope out of his pocket. Linden flashed the tickets in her face.

"We're going—I'll get to see Anita Baker, Najee, Alex Bugnon, and Nick Colionne & Ledisi—live!" she cried out.

"Yes, Air Supply, Dionne Warwick, and Michael Bolton are also performing tonight, Shay."

"Yes!" She shouted, and started doing the happy dance around the table.

"What time is the Jazz concert?"

"It starts at six o'clock."

"What! It's three o'clock, now. That leaves me with just three hours to get ready," she said, after glancing at the brass clock.

Linden burst out laughing.

"Three hours is plenty of time to get dressed Shay."

"Yes, for a man, but I have to find something to wear. I'm in desperate need of a manicure, pedicure, and I need my hair done," she whined, threading her fingers through her long, thick, tangled hair. "Three hours is *not* enough time, Linden!"

The sudden knock at the door startled, Shay. She snatched up her robe off the floor and slipped back into it.

"I have another surprise for you," he said, slipping into his own robe.

He opened the door and admitted four women.

"Sweetheart, these ladies are here to make you look even more beautiful than you are now. I have two nail technicians, a hairstylist, and the owner of Gabriella, the dress shop where women from all over St. Lucia come to buy her fashion, so I've been told," Linden stated.

The ladies entered the suite, each loaded down with their equipment and dresses.

"I'll let you ladies get to work," he said, easing out of the room.

"Linden," Shay called out to him, before he reached the bedroom door.

"Yes, sweetheart, what is it?"

"I'll never forget this!"

"You can thank me later after the jazz festival," he whispered with a sexy tone in his voice. The wicked gleam in his eyes told her a simple kiss would not be enough.

"You have a date, Mr. Stewart."

He walked into the bedroom with a big grin on his face.

"Ma'am, we don't have much time. Your husband is taking you to the concert, tonight?" Celia, the nail technician happily asked, after introducing herself.

"Yes!"

"You want to dazzle him, tonight?" Renee inquired.

"I want to look my best," Shay said, but she didn't reveal to the ladies that Linden wasn't her husband.

While Celia worked on her hands, Teresa worked on her toes, and Renee who introduced herself as the owner of Gabriella, showed Shay all colors and style of dresses to wear.

She finally selected a coral, fitted, sheath dress because it was elegant, and it accentuated her curves. She had a pair of sandals and handbag that would match the dress perfectly in her suitcase. That climb up Petit Piton Mountain yesterday added a glowing color to her already sun-kissed, caramel complexion.

"Ma'am, you've selected the perfect dress for your body. I'll take it down to the shop to be pressed, and now Sofia is ready to whip your hair into something wonderful."

Chapter Five

Linden, clad in black pants and a coral shirt, stood beside the chauffeured Lincoln Town Car he hired for the evening, awaiting Shay. She wanted to surprise him, so she forced him to dress in the living room. Then she banished him from his suite.

Shay stepped out of the resort an hour later looking elegant in a coral sheath. Her ebony curls were piled on top of her head, and ringlets of curls graced her forehead and her nape. Her makeup was a minimal, green liner under her eyes, two coats of ebony mascara on her already long straight eyelashes, blush on her cheeks, and on her lips she wore ruby-red lipstick. She wore a simple gold rope necklace. Diamond-cut, gold, one-inch, earrings dangled from her ears.

Shay sashayed over to Linden, smiling at his handsome appearance.

Linden's shirt not only matched her sheath, it called attention to his newly golden tan. His grin was irresistibly. He was devastatingly attractive, tonight. She was almost tempted to skip the jazz festival, drag him into his suite, strip him down to his birthday suit, and jump his bones. But she wanted to see Anita Baker and Najee perform, so she got into the awaiting car.

Linden slid in besides her, the driver started the engine, and they rode down that mountain heading toward the concert. Shay slid into his arms and threaded her fingers through his thick hair.

"Where did you get that shirt, Linden?"

"Renee told me it would match your dress. So, I purchased it."

"We're looking like this was perfectly arranged," Shay cooed into his ear.

Linden kissed Shay's lips, tasting strawberry from her lip gloss. He wanted a deeper taste from those sweet lips of hers.

"Mmm, why don't we go back to my suite?"

"*Absolutely* not, Mr. Linden David Stewart!"

"Then, I suggest you don't sit too close to me. Otherwise, I'll take you *right* here in this car," Linden groaned. Deeply aroused, he threaded his fingers through his hair. He still had to make it through the jazz concert.

Shay's eyes slid down to the seat of his pants and noticed his arousal there.

"*Down boy*, I promise to take care of you, tonight," she said, and she licked her lips.

Linden's eyes filled with desire. Shay moved away from him and sat on the opposite side of the car, fanning herself with her purse.

§

The audience was hyped, clapping, and swaying to the beat of Air Supply. Linden and Shay sat in the fifth row, in the middle tier of an amphitheater—an oval arena set up on Pigeon Island—in the middle of the park. They were among thousands of people of all ethnic backgrounds. It was obvious that Linden must have paid good money for those seats. There were people in VIP tents watching the concert on monitors, and others sprawled on the grass on blankets just listening to the show. However, Linden and Shay had practically front row seats. The sound system was impressive, and Shay couldn't hear a word Linden had said to her in the last few minutes. She pointed to her ears and shook her head to let him know she couldn't hear him.

Linden shook his head in acknowledgment that Shay couldn't possibly hear him over the music. He grabbed her right hand and kissed her palm.

A gentle moan of passion escaped her lips. That kiss on her palm sent a flame straight down to her femininity. Shay stared into his eyes until the crowd roared again, and her eyes returned to the stage.

Michael Bolton took center stage with a medley of some of his greatest hits. He wooed the women in the crowd with his signature song, "When A Man Loves A Woman." His tenor voice belted through the speakers. The St. Lucian natives shouted with pride when he concluded with a reggae piece, "Said I Loved You…But I lied." They sang with him and danced to the beat of the drums.

The highlight of the festival for Shay was when Anita Baker graced the stage. She looked stunning in an elegant but simple black sleeveless jumpsuit and her fierce, sassy short haircut. Diamond stud earrings sparkled on her ears.

Anita serenaded the audience for over an hour with the melodies of her romantic songs. She began with "Sweet Love," "Caught Up In The Rapture," "You Belong To Me," and ended her first set with "Giving You The Best That I Got." The crowd wouldn't let her leave, so she came back onstage and sang "You Bring Me Joy," "Fairy Tales," and "Body and Soul."

Shay and Linden, along with the other couples, swayed to her strong, supple alto voice as Anita created a cocoon of love flowing all around them. The crowd was hyped, and when Anita tried to leave the stage for a second time, they gave a thunderous applause and cried out for more.

A gracious, Baker, came back onstage for an encore, and she called Dionne Warwick and Angie Stone to join her. Together, they sang more of her classic songs. Tears slid down Shay's cheeks because she would never forget this moment with Linden.

The jazz explosion consisting of Najee, Alex Bugnon, Nick Colionne & Ledisi joined them and their performance was awesome. It took Shay's breath away. Shay took off her three-inch sandals, and dance with the audience to "Touch of Heaven," "Betcha Don't Know," and "Now That I've Found You."

Linden stood back, and watched Shay's ass sensuously gyrate to the music. He fantasized about all of the positions he intended to incorporate in his making love to her later that night.

§

Hours later, winding down after the jazz festival, Linden lay in bed waiting for Shay to give him his special treat. He lay on his back with his legs spread wide apart stroking his rapidly growing erection.

If she didn't get in there soon, he'll burst, he thought.

"Shay!"

"Be patient...I'm coming!"

"Sweetheart, I'm cumming...without you!" He groaned as pre-cum ejaculated from the head of his very ready cock.

Shay, clad in a red lace teddy sashayed into the bedroom with a soup bowl in her hands.

"Hey! Stop that," she complained. Her lips drooped sensuously at each corner.

"*I'm* supposed to be doing that."

She slapped his hands and immediately drizzled something warm—a white, milky substance—all over Linden's stomach. It oozed down his flat abs, collected on the head of his swollen manhood, and slid down both of his thighs.

"What the *hell?*" Linden tried to bolt out of bed, but Shay's palms pressed against his chest, and held him in place.

"I'm not going to hurt you, Linden."

"What have you done?"

"It's white-chocolate, and I'm going to lick every drop, Mr. Stewart." Her voice managed to sound even sexier than normal. "So, lie back, close your eyes, and enjoy your treat."

"You're going to drive me crazy, Shay!"

"Did I tell you how much I enjoyed tonight?"

"Mmm," he said, after swiping his thumb across the head of his sex. He sucked off every drop of the chocolate. "White chocolate—like me," Linden said, just above a whisper.

"White boy...you're the first to sample my body."

"I'll be your *only* white boy to dip into your milk chocolate," he said, adamantly.

Shay placed the bowl on the nightstand and smiled down at her handiwork.

"You're getting a little *possessive*, Linden."

"And you've kept me waiting long enough, Shay. Finish this!"

"Did your mother ever tell you that you need to buy some patience?"

"*All* the time." His grin was irresistible.

What a charmer, she thought.

Meticulously, Shay's tongue skimmed over his skin like hot-liquid-fire. Her sweet tongue slid up one thigh, then the other, greedily licking up the white chocolate. She left his pulsating sex for last, licking all sides at first, and slid under to collect the chocolate covering his balls.

§

Shay's tongue was driving Linden crazy. He nearly bolted off the bed when her tongue lapped at his sensitive balls. Her fingers were very gentle, but he'd never allowed any women to handle his family jewels— his lifeline. Then, she deep throated as much as she could capture of his erect cock. Her teeth were gentle; yet, it scraped his flesh one minute, and massaged him the next.

"S-h-a-y!" he groaned.

Linden's body bucked against the mattress. His fingers threaded through her elegant coiffure as he rode his orgasm. By his second orgasm, the pins from Shay's hair had tumbled out, one-by-one, falling onto the bed and the floor. Looking sexy as all hell, her hair tumbled down her silky shoulders, and her lips were swollen from sucking him.

Shay fell across his hips trying to regain her breath. Deeply, she breathed in until her eyes swept across Linden's moist body. She couldn't believe he was still aroused. His sex expanded right before her eyes once again.

That man's cock is never flaccid, she thought.

In the blink of an eye, Linden peeled off Shay's damp teddy. He nudged her on her back, and his knees spread her thighs apart to accommodate him.

His eyes scanned down her alluring body. How did he find this stunning, passionate treasure?

"Now…babe!" she ordered, writhing her body into the bed.

Linden smiled down at her. He kept her waiting as she had done him earlier.

He wanted her to anticipate his next move.

He wanted her desire for him to be at a feverish pace.

He wanted her pussy quivering and creaming, just for him.

He wanted

"L-i-n-d-e-n!" she wailed, needing her release this century.

Their eyes locked, and sexual fever laced their bodies.

He thrusted into her body with a passion he'd never felt with any other woman. His tempo, slow and easy, then fast and deep, hitting every one of her erotic zones, until that sweet-sensual-ripple from her wet hot pussy clenched his rod, and sapped him of his strength.

§

"Thank you for taking me to the jazz festival." Shay's voice was now hoarse from screaming out Linden's name. Tears of happiness slid down her cheeks. "No one has ever given me such a treat."

Their naked bodies still moist from lovemaking, Linden's thumb wiped her tears.

"I *wanted* to do that for you. Thank you for my special treat. No woman has ever done that for me."

"No woman has ever gone down on you?"

"Not with white chocolate, and not quite so deliciously as with those sexy lips of yours, Shay."

"Mmm," she moaned. Her hands slid between their sticky bodies.

"We've created quite a mess! White chocolate is all over the bedding and our bodies, Shay."

"Are you complaining now, Mr. Stewart?"

"Absolutely not; but we should take a shower, sweetheart."

"I can't move...tomorrow... morning," she moaned, closing her eyes and drifting to sleep.

"Shay?"

The sounds of a light snore escaped her lips.

"Tomorrow, it will be," he said softly. His palms cupped the cheeks of her ass, bringing him deeper into her heat.

Linden's eyes closed. He loved the feel of being enveloped within Shay's moist folds. Their sexes unprotected once again, as he too drifted off to sleep.

Chapter Six

By noon, Shay dragged Linden out of the resort to do something she loved: shopping. St. Lucia's downtown market was like a large, open flea market selling everything from fruits, vegetables, and hot prepared foods, such as vegetables, fish cakes, roti, Dhal pies, and cherry juice. She found island fabrics, hand woven hats and baskets, seed necklace, earrings, and other indigenous woven crafts.

She met an elderly woman who was selling baskets out of the back of her truck. She told Shay that the woven crafts she saw in the market were made from a local hanging root called "aralie," and it grew on the island. Shay purchased an oval basket for her kitchen.

Shay fell in love with the charm of the Creole people. They were very friendly and spoke English and French patois. She found their native tongue sexy to her ears. They walked from one stall to the next, and she was like a kid in a candy store oohing and ahing at what she saw.

It was very humid as was the norm, there on the island. The sun kissed her face once again. She slid on her burgundy baseball cap, and sun shades to protect her skin and eyes. Linden's Ray-Ban sunglasses covered his eyes, and the sunscreen which he slathered on his golden skin earlier was all he needed.

The smell of fish frying and the sweet scent of overripe fruits perfumed the air as she shopped for gifts. Shay wanted to purchase a piece of island jewelry for Nia and Tatiana, a little trinket for two of her co-workers, along with some items to decorate her studio apartment. Over the years, every time she traveled to an exotic island, she picked up a trinket for her memory collection. She was still searching for that.

Four hours later, Linden was ready to head back to his suite. He was loaded down with Shay's purchases. He didn't complain the whole time and stood by patiently when she haggled over the price for a necklace she wanted to purchase. Linden offered to pay for it, but she cut her eyes at him, so he backed off and left her to negotiate the price.

Linden couldn't wait to unload Shay's purchases in his suite. He wanted an ice cold Sam Adams beer. Instead, he spotted a stall with a big bold sign. It read: ST. LUCIA'S FINEST PITON BEER. As Shay haggled over the piece of jewelry, he walked over to another stall and placed an American twenty dollar bill in the merchant's hand for a bottle of beer. He chugged it down in less than thirty seconds. The beer went down smoothly and tasted good to his parched throat. By the fourth beer, he was feeling mellow.

"Do you like this necklace, Linden?" Shay inquired. She turned around to discover that he was no longer by her side.

Shay spotted him a few feet away at a refreshment booth—with a beer in his hands. Her purchases were at his feet. Several of them had fallen out of the bag, she noticed.

She gave the woman a ten dollar bill.

"Yuh cousin will like," the woman said in her musical lilt. She had the biggest grin on her round face.

I just paid too much money for Tatiana's necklace.

Sauntering over to Linden, Shay dropped the necklace into her canvas bag. She picked up the spilled items and slid them back into the shopping bags.

"Hey you, how are you doing?" She asked, removing the beer out of Linden's hands, and taking a gulp of the Piton beer.

"Mmm, this tastes pretty good."

Linden's hand curved around her waist. Naughtily, he palmed her ass and pressed her into his erection. "I want you," he slurred.

"How many beers did you drink?"

"I'm famished, sweetheart!"

His fingers slid under her shorts and stroked her ass.

"Linden!" she smacked at his hands. "Come, let's get you back to the suite."

Shay picked up their bags, handed him a few, and slipped her arm around his waist. She led him away from the shoppers.

~ 55 ~

"Babe, you're a little tipsy from drinking beer on an empty stomach, Linden."

"Are you chastising me?"

"No, I just want to get us back to the suite."

"And I want to *fuck* that sweet-juicy ass of yours, until you can't walk," he growled.

"Sure, anything you want, babe. Let's just get back to the resort," she said as they exited the market.

A taxi pulled right up in front of the entrance to the market.

"Yuh want a taxi," a young man in a red St Lucia T-shirt called out to them, getting up from the driver's seat.

"Yes!" Shay said, grateful for his assistance as he opened the passenger door. He relieved her of her purchases, and she took Linden's bags and passed it to him.

"Damn, it's hot!" he groaned as he sat in the back seat. He unfastened the top three buttons of his white dress shirt.

"You can take a shower when we get back to the resort."

"Hmm, sounds delicious. Will you join me?"

Linden kissed her right cheek. His fingers trailed under her T-shirt to play with her bra clasps.

"Linden!"

She slapped his hands.

The driver sat back in his seat. "Where to, ma'am?" the young man inquired.

"The Jade Mountain Resort," Shay stated quickly.

"There's a hundred dollar tip if you get us there in fifteen minutes," Linden said. His left hand palmed Shay's right breast.

"Yes, sir. I'll have you there in a snap!"

The taxi driver pulled onto the road. From his rear view mirror he watched the pretty woman constantly slapped at the white man's wandering hands. He chuckled to himself, knowing what was going on.

Twenty minutes later, Shay guided a staggering Linden into the bedroom. He fell across the bed.

"Shit, those Piton beers are pretty potent," he said, before passing out cold.

Shay removed his shoes and slid the blanket over him.

"Yeah, pretty potent, I say." Shay was heated in more ways than one. She looked down at a snoring Linden. "I guess I'll be showering, alone."

§

That night, they returned to The Pulse Club where they first met and danced — if what they did could be called that. Instead of going to the dance floor, Shay climbed on top of Linden and gave him a lap dance — right in his seat.

"What are you doing?" he hissed.

Linden looked to the right and left of him because Shay's body blocked his front view. He noticed everyone's eyes were now glued to them, and they were the center of attention.

Anita Baker's song, "Sweet Love," played in the background.

Shay threaded her fingers through his hair, knowing that would drive him wild. She gyrated her body against Linden's, rocking and grinding her pulsating core closer to his, in perfects synch with the music. The tent in the seam of his pants couldn't be missed as Shay brushed against it. It throbbed against her dewy crotch, and she wrapped her legs encircling them.

"Shay, don't do this—not *here!*" He groaned, watching their *captive* audience.

He took deep breaths. Perspiration beaded his face, and mopped his sweaty forehead.

After another series of gyrations against him, Linden's dick was hard as a rock. He couldn't take it any longer. He was ready to blow!

"Oooh!" She cried out suddenly.

Shay tried to suppress her giggles when Linden removed her legs from around his trembling body.

He tossed her over his left shoulder, and marched toward the entrance of the club. Pressing his way through the throng of people, Linden noticed several of the men's eyes bulging. Their tongues hung out of their mouth. They salivated as if Shay were dessert—she was his dessert. Linden had no intention of fighting his way out of that club. No other man but him would taste her body.

§

The second they entered the bedroom, Linden backed Shay against the wall. His fingers ripped at her lace thong, and his pants in his lustful need to get inside of her. He still pulsated from the lap dance she had given him at The Pulse Club. He didn't know how he was able to restrain himself. He was seconds away from spilling his seed—right there in that club. In retaliation, he most certainly was going to get his right now.

"Linden...the bed, babe. Wouldn't the bed be more comfortable?" She cried out in pleasure, hitching her legs around his waist.

"No bed." Linden bit her ear. "Right here—right now, Shay!"

He took her there, right against the wall. The piston-driving strength of his body possessed hers. Giving back as well as she got, Shay arched to meet his thrusts.

Their eyes locked. There was an unspoken challenge in the depths of Linden's violet eyes.

No one could stroke the flames in her succulent core like Linden. His thrusts were deep and hard, and Shay cried out from his relentless tempo. He made love to her with a ravenous intensity until she cried out, abandoning herself to the multiple climaxes spiraling throughout her body. His love's sweet lava flowed like warm honey.

Later, Shay lay in Linden's arms contented with life. There time was quickly coming to a close. After tomorrow they would each get on an airplane and head back to their respective lives.

§

Their last evening in St. Lucia, Linden ordered a romantic candlelight dinner for two. Reggie set up the meal beside the pool. It was a five-course meal, champagne, soups and salads, grilled chateaubriand, red snapper, sweet and sour pork chop island style and all of the trimmings. For dessert, there were caramel bananas, and a coconut pie with vanilla crème anglaise.

The candlelight surrounding the pool bounced off the iridescent reflective tiles when Linden dimmed the lights, setting the mood for romance. He even filled the suite with three dozen red roses in his effort to make their last evening together perfect.

Shay sashayed into the living room dressed in a sheer, black negligee, leaving nothing to his imagination. Her satiny skin glimmered through the fabric like liquid caramel. Smiling, she sighed at the handsome gentleman seated before her.

She scanned the room and noticed that lit candles were everywhere as well as fresh red roses.

He did this for me, she thought.

"Sweetheart...you look good enough to eat," he growled.

I have been sampling Linden's body for the last six nights and tonight's love making promises to be hotter than the last, she thought.

Linden's eyes bucked. Her goodies were now on display thanks to the translucence of her sexy nightie. His eyes slid up her body, slowly taking inventory of her shapely legs, the apex of her thighs, and her caramel-satiny skin peeking through. Desirable, inviting, and beckoning him—her nipples were taut, her wet-luscious lips open, and those eyes...He forced himself not to stretch her body out on the dining table, minus the five-course meal, and to thrust into her juicy tunnel then. He decided to dine first and save his energy for later.

Instead, Linden took her right hand and kissed the tips of her long fingers.

"I've ordered your favorites," he said, smiling down at her.

He led her over to the table, pulled out her chair, and helped her into the seat. He kissed the pulse point at the base of her neck, shook out her napkin, and dropped it on her lap before pushing her chair closer to the table. Then, he sat down in his seat.

The thought of never seeing him again made Shay want to cry. She pushed her dinner from one side of the plate to the other. She couldn't eat. None of the food interested her.

"Shay, is there something *wrong* with your dinner?" Linden inquired after watching her for the last five minutes.

"No, it's delicious as usual, babe. I'm just not hungry."

She gazed into his sparkling eyes. Her voice came out in a broken tone. "I'm going to miss you!"

A lone tear slid down her cheek. Shay had already admitted to herself that she had fallen in love with a man not of her own complexion. He was easy to talk to, made love deliciously—pleasuring her first and them himself. Foreplay and dirty talk whispered into her ear increased her desire for him. How could she *possibly* return to Philly *without* him?

"I'm going to miss you too, Shay," he said, reading her thoughts. "I'll visit you in Philadelphia."

"*Will* you?" she asked, excited. He didn't want to end their time together.

"Yes, I will."

"You don't have to *lie* to me, Linden."

"I'm not lying, sweetheart."

"I know this is *only* an island fling." She intoned.

"Shay, is that what you think we are?"

"I don't know how *you* feel, Linden, but I've never felt this way with any other man," she confessed openly for the second time.

Why do I disclose so much of myself? she wondered to herself.

"I'll call you and we'll get together I promise! Now, don't spoil our last evening together. Eat up because you'll need the energy. I plan to screw your socks off!"

"You're so horny, but I love it."

§

After dinner, Linden's sexual appetite was insatiable.

Their eyes locked and held.

His kisses were like sweet nectar to Shay's tongue, and she drank deeply.

They met each other's needs as if it would be their last time together. Linden entered her haven as if there were an outside force pushing him. He drove into her body again and again.

Shay's legs climbed up his back, pushing him deeper into her pulsating wetness. The sac of his balls — hot and wet from her dripping cunt, slapped her ass when he rode her with unabashed fervor. The head of his cock scraped the tip of her womb; her love muscles gripped him — contracted around him, again and again, until they both exploded into a million pieces.

Hours later, sleep eluded Shay. Her ass pressed against his sex. Linden's arms encircled her waist, his heart beating against her back. Totally satisfied, he snored softly in her ears.

I'll miss moments like this, being wrapped in his arms, she thought.

Shay wanted Linden's desire for her to last forever. If he asked her to come home with him, she would. There was nothing nothing holding her in Philly, except her two favorite cousins. She was a junior accountant for a small finance company, but the job was just a paycheck. Three nights a week, she attended a community college, and she was just ten credits shy of receiving her Bachelor's degree, in accounting. She *wanted* more — *needed* more, and Michael's deception just left her vulnerable to *more* hurt. In her heart, Linden was the one!

Could their island fling spill over into their real life? Was he being completely honest when he said he'd visit her?

All of those thoughts ran through Shay's mind and kept her awake. Eventually, she drifted off to sleep.

Just before dawn, Shay was awakened when Linden entered her body again—filling her with his hot, pulsating cock. She didn't protest when he got careless. He'd forgotten to put on a condom once again. For some reason, she felt this time was *really* goodbye.

Chapter Seven

Shay's flight was set to depart at ten A.M., Saturday morning so Linden ordered a car to take her to the airport. They were dressed to return to the real world: she, in jeans and a black leather jacket, and he, in a suit jacket and jeans. They stood in front of the car wrapped in each other's arms, as Linden caressed her back.

"I *hate* goodbyes," she whispered into his chest, inhaling his smell. She'd never forget the scent of Cool Water cologne. His clean and refreshing smell filled her with a sense of peace and tranquility, just like the island of St. Lucia. The blend of musk and sandalwood made her want to strip him right there, and make love to him *one* final time.

"This isn't goodbye, Shay. I won't let it be. I'll call you tonight, and we can try out phone sex," he whispered in her ear.

"Phone sex, you're crazy, Linden."

"I'm *crazy* about *you*, Shay!"

"And, I'm crazy about you, too!"

Shay pushed out of his arms and reluctantly climbed into the car.

"Have a safe flight. Call me; I'll be waiting by the phone," she said, tears welling up in her eyes.

Linden wiped at the tears spilling down her cheeks.

"Don't cry, sweetheart. I have something for you." He reached into his suit jacket, and pulled out a small black, velvet box. "Don't open it until I call you tonight, Shay."

He kissed her wet, trembling lips. Then, his thumbs wiped her cheeks again. He stared into her sometimes green, sometimes golden brown eyes.

I can get lost in those eyes for the rest of my life, he thought.

"Tonight," he said, smiling.

Linden shut the door. He slapped the hood of the car with the palm of his left hand, signaling the driver to take off. He bent his head to hide his own teary eyes. His hands trembled when he eased them into his denim pockets. He sauntered back into the resort, as if their parting didn't affect him.

Tears streamed down Shay's cheeks as she watched Linden disappeared into the resort. She crossed her right hand against her breasts. Her heartbeat was erratic, and she sighed from the emotions curdling inside of her.

"I love you!" she finally admitted as the Jade Mountain Resort whizzed by in the background.

§

Two hours later, Shay took her first class seat on the jet and Michael was already seated and having a drink. He was really enjoying the amenities of flying in first class.

"I thought you were going to miss this flight, Shay!"

"I'm here," she hissed disgusted because she was seated next to the idiot.

"How was your island fling?" he snickered.

"And how was your island *slut?*" she retaliated.

"It *takes* one to *know* one," he added, a nasty undertone in his voice.

"When we get home, I want you and all of your shit out of my apartment. Enjoy the rest of this flight, because your free-loading days are over!" That said, Shay asked the flight attendant to change her seat. She couldn't *possibly* sit next to him for the next four and a half hours.

"You're ending our good thing because of *him?*" Michael asked, reeking of alcohol.

What had she seen in Michael for the last three years? Shay wondered.

"We're *finished*," she countered, ice etching her tone.

The flight attendant found a seat for her in coach. She slept her headache away, clutching the black velvet box Linden had given. She missed him already, and she couldn't wait for his phone call, later that evening.

§

Linden boarded the company jet and could've kicked himself for not asking Shay to join him. He could've easily instructed the pilot to drop her off in Philadelphia first, and then swing back into Baltimore/Washington International Airport.

But I didn't, he thought.

Things were moving a little too fast for him. He'd never felt this way about any woman, so he needed to *pump* the brakes, and slow things down.

Linden didn't lie to Shay when he said he would call her. He had every intention of pursuing a relationship with her, but he needed to *think*. Yesterday, while she was having a massage, he went down to the jewelry store looking for a gift for Shay. The platinum pendant he purchased for her wasn't a goodbye gift — more like "an until we meet again gift." The diamond star pendant reminded him of Shay. She was a quiet storm: warm-hearted, beautiful and passionate in his arms.

Her kisses were sweeter than Godiva chocolate. When he penetrated her succulent core, the way her pussy insistently clenched him, drove him wild. He loved the way her long talons clawed his back, and how she cried out his name when he came — spilling his lifeline.

Shay has branded me for life, he thought.

Sexually, they were compatible. Intellectuality, she could hold her own — although, she was a bookkeeper for a small finance company. They liked the same kind of music, and in seven days he knew his heart. He could've committed to Shay before she boarded that plane. In fact, he had requested a custom piece to match the diamond star pendant. The designer was local, so Linden commissioned him to make the matching ring to the two-carat diamond pendant.

Linden could hear his father telling him that anything that's worth having would wait for him. *If Shay is the woman for me, God will keep her, until we meet again.*

"Mr. Stewart," Wendy greeted.

Linden looked up at the smiling face of the company's flight attendant.

"Would you like anything to drink before takeoff, sir?"

"No, Wendy. I think I'll just take a nap."

"You look refreshed and relaxed, sir. Did you enough your vacation?"

"I must say, I've enjoyed my time on St. Lucia," he said. His mouth curved into an unconscious smile.

"We'll be taking off soon. Please fasten your seatbelt."

Linden fastened his seatbelt and gazed out the window. Shay should've been halfway home by now, he told himself. He leaned back in his seat and closed his eyes. The memories of her straddling his hips and riding him aroused him, but he drifted off to sleep.

§

Linden tossed his luggage into the trunk of his yellow Hummer. He whizzed out of the airport parking lot. He was in a hurry to get home and to call Shay.

His right hand turned on the radio, and his left hand held the steering wheel as he took the ramp at the speed of twenty miles an hour, instead of the minimum ten. The Baltimore-Washington Parkway was bumper-to-bumper traffic as he eased into the middle lane. Anita Baker's song, "Sweet Love," crooned to him. His thoughts lingered on that special night after the jazz festival.

Shay dripped warm, white chocolate all over his lower body. Her lips had tried to suck him dry. She fell back on his stomach inhaling deeply until he was erect again.

Linden noted the surprised look on Shay's face when his rod stood at rapt attention. He was thinking of the lonely nights ahead when she would no longer warm his bed. He reversed their positions, unrelentingly thrusting into her pussy—once, twice and a third time, until he exploded flooding her vaginal walls. Shay purred like a sated kitten. He loved the cry of passion from her sweet lips as she climaxed and her pussy spasms held him prisoner.

Shay can hold me prisoner for the rest of my life.

Feverishly, they made love again until he fell asleep with the biggest grin on his face.

The screech of tires and the smell of burning rubber brought him out of his musing. The sudden downpour made driving on the parkway slippery, and his vehicle went into a tailspin. With both hands griping the steering wheels, Linden fought for control of his Hummer.

Oh God, I'm going to hit that tanker truck ahead!

"Shay!" Linden cried out, seconds before the crash.

Chapter Eight

"Linden!" Shay cried out not knowing that he was calling out to her, as well.

She bolted off the sofa, trembling. A shiver passed over her. Dazed, she looked around her living room. The television was blaring. It was three A.M., on Sunday morning. She had fallen asleep on the sofa with her cordless telephone in her hands, waiting for Linden's call.

"He *never* called," she said out loud.

Disappointed, Shay dialed his home and cell phone for the fifth time. Both calls went straight to voicemail. Angry, she walked into her bedroom, stripped down to her bare flesh, and eased into bed.

Stupid! Stupid! Stupid! She thought, taunting herself.

Shay beat on her pillow as if she were hitting Linden's body. She was angry with him and herself for believing they could possibly be *more* than an island fling. Tears fell down her cheeks when she finally lay her head on the pillow.

Seconds later, she jumped out of the bed, remembering the black velvet box Linden slipped into her hands on her way to the airport. He asked her not to open it until he called her. She went in the living room searching for it. It slid into the cushion of her sofa when she had fallen asleep. She opened the box.

A platinum diamond star pendant was boldly displayed inside of the box. It was exquisite, and the weight of the diamond was at least a carat and a half. She took the pendant and placed it on her neck. She felt closer to Linden when she rubbed it. He seemed sincere when he said he'd call her that night. They were going to try out phone sex.

There has to be a reason for him not calling me, she thought.

She lay back down, but her mind returned to her tortured thinking: Linden *never* called. Tears slid down Shay's cheeks. She gripped the diamond pendant as memories of their making love replayed in her head, until she drifted back to sleep.

§

When Shay woke up on Sunday afternoon, she called him and left several more messages. He still did not return her calls. She held the pendant against her neck and finally realized the present was really a goodbye gift.

He lied to me.

Tears slid down her cheeks. It was *really* over between them!

§

Linden didn't want her, and Michael wouldn't give up. She packed up his things—stuffs he left at her apartment over the past three years. Although, he took the box without a fuss Michael told Shay he wasn't giving up on them. In fact, he dropped by her office that Monday and invited her out to lunch, but she wouldn't budge. The first week back home, he continued to call her every night, but the only person she wanted to see or talk to was Linden.

For the next three weeks, Shay just went with the flow—dragging herself to work and eating very little. She had no appetite for food, stupidly; she continued to reach out to Linden. She called and left messages on his cell, at his office, and his home phone, but he never returned *any* of her calls.

Shay cut herself off from everyone, including her cousins Nia and Tatiana. She screened her telephone calls and never returned them. Michael had finally given up on her and moved on. She lost herself in music, and she couldn't stand to listen to Anita Baker's voice any longer without seeing Linden. Sade's sultry tones ministered to her broken heart. She kept playing that song, "An Ordinary Love." The lyrics, "You…brightened…every…day…with…your…sweet…smile."

She looked out of her lonely, seventh-floor apartment window and cried. "I…keep… crying…for…you…," cooed in her ears. Her own tears slid down her cheeks and soaked her negligee. Many nights, she went to bed with those lyrics, in her head—dreaming of Linden as he passionately made love to her.

§

Saturday morning, she woke up to the sound of someone banging at her apartment door.

"I know you're home, Shay!" Tatiana hollered. "Open this door, right now, or I'll call the police! You've avoided my calls for three weeks, and I'm *not* going away. Let me in!"

Shay was surprised her cousin hadn't planted herself at her door before now. She had to let her inside, because Tatiana wasn't leaving. She was a tenacious, five-foot, ball of fire. What Tatiana *wanted*—she *got*. If she was determined to get inside, she would call the police to gain access to Shay's apartment.

Tatiana breezed through the door and plopped down on the sofa the moment Shay let her in.

"It's balmy outside, cuz," Tatiana said. Her voice was warm and bubbly.

She watched Shay, dressed in a skimpy, purple negligee, crawl back on the other end of the sofa—cuddled under the blanket as if she were cold.

"It's warm and toasty in here. Are you ill?"

"Nope!"

What's up? It's noon. Do you plan to get dressed, today?"

"No!"

"You've been avoiding Nia and my calls since your return from St. Lucia, Shay. Nia had to work today; otherwise, she would've been here with me. What's going on?"

"I just wanted to be left *alone*, okay."

~ 73 ~

"I saw Michael with that skank, Miranda Jones. They were in Club Champagne, and she was giving him a lap dance like you wouldn't believe. She would've allowed him to ball her, right there, in the middle of the dance floor," Tatiana said, to get a rise out of her cousin.

"Michael and I are no longer dating. He can ball any woman he chooses."

"Praise God!" Tatiana bolted off the sofa, elated about that bit of news.

"I've been trying to get you to end it with that dog for three years. What made you see the light?"

Shay gave Tatiana the "evil eyes" hoping she would back off. But she knew it was useless.

Tatiana slipped back on the sofa. She pulled out her nail file and started to shape her nails. She had nowhere she needed to be. Sooner or later, she figured that Shay would start talking.

"Two days into my vacation, I caught him in bed with an island slut," Shay confessed, eventually.

"*What?*"

"Do you know Michael had the nerve to screw her in my hotel bed? I paid for that trip. I thought it would be a romantic getaway for us," Shay said. Her blood boiled when she thought back on the three years, she wasted with that *snake*.

"I can't *believe* he'd be stupid enough to cheat on you in St. Lucia—right underneath your nose," Tatiana replied.

"He's arrogant enough to believe he could get away with it. The challenge must have made it even sweeter for him," Shay said, rancor sharpened her voice.

"So, you're moping around here because of him. Let's go out and get two Philly Cheesesteaks. I'm starving!"

Shay groaned at the thought of biting into a greasy Philly Cheesesteak.

"I'm not hungry, and I'm *not* moping over Michael."

"It looks to me like you are!"

"No, I'm not. I went to a club in St. Lucia and picked up a man," Shay admitted.

Tatiana dropped her nail file. "Tell me...tell me, more," she said, smiling at Shay—who also had a big grin on her face.

"The sex was incredible, and his smoldering violet eyes..."

"His smoldering, violet eyes—don't tell me you picked up a *white* boy, in St. Lucia, Shay?"

"Yes, I did it with a *white* boy. I rode him, and he rode my black ass, too!"

"You-you let him do you in the *ass?* How *could* you? You wouldn't even allow Michael to touch *that.*"

"Linden was different. He's a gentle lover; a giving-passionate man. It felt natural—right in his arms. He swept me away and believe me Tee, I *wanted* to be swept away," she mumbled, tears once again sliding down her cheeks.

"Girl, I've never seen you this way. Now you're mooning over this guy, Linden?"

"I *need* him. I *love* him, Tee!"

"You're just an island fling to him, cuz!"

"No, I won't and don't believe that."

"Has he called you since you returned home, Shay?"

"No, he hasn't called me as he promised. But he will."

Look, Linden gave me *this*," Shay said, extending out her pendant in Tatiana's direction.

~ 75 ~

Tatiana's eyes lit up to the diamond, star pendant gracing Shay's neck.

"He paid a pretty penny for that," Tatiana declared.

She knew her jewelry. The brilliant color and the shine reflecting from the diamonds said it all.

"He spends money like water, Tatiana."

"That's a goodbye gift, Shay!"

"It *wasn't* a *goodbye* gift."

"Shay...Michael hurt you, and Linden will do the same if you don't wise up. Besides, it can't be anything more, and you need to give your love to a brother!"

"When you fall in love Tee, it isn't with the color of a man's skin. I fell in love with him. Our souls connected. Linden's a passionate lover, and we revealed personal, intimate details about ourselves. He spent a lot of money on tickets for the last night of the jazz festival. His gift to me was a manicure, a pedicure, a hairstylist, and he purchased a dress for me that evening."

"You said he spends money like water. That gift doesn't prove a thing."

"But he did it for me! No *one* has *ever* done that for me," Shay said, as she slapped her chest. "He's here," she said pointing to her heart. "I'll admit it was a one-night stand that led to seven days of sexual bliss. I love him, Tatiana, and I know he loves me!"

"It's been three weeks since you've returned. Why hasn't he called you?" Tatiana questioned. Her tone was as gentle as it could be. Her cousin was heading for a big fall.

"I don't know," Shay mumbled, tears rolling down her cheeks.

§

Two weeks later, Shay passed out at work. It was a Wednesday morning, and she was escorted down to the nurse's office. The nurse suggested Shay make an appointment with her family doctor. Shay didn't *need* to see her doctor. All she needed was some rest; so she left work early that day, and climbed into bed. Linden invaded her dreams, and all she *really* needed was a decent night's sleep.

Thursday morning, as she prepared for work, her eyes glanced over at the calendar and noticed the date. Shay realized she'd missed her last monthly cycle, and she *could* be pregnant.

Instead of going to work, she walked over to the nearest pharmacy and brought a popular home pregnancy test. She seen the commercial on television and it was supposed to be accurate and quick. Shay *needed* to know *now* if she was carrying Linden's baby.

§

In hours, Shay had her results.
Damn! How could I have been so stupid?
She was pregnant. The test had confirmed that, and Linden was avoiding all of her calls. Things weren't going to go down like that. First, Michael dogged her, and now Linden. He *would* be *accountable* for his actions!
We created this baby together, and he'll see me!

Chapter Nine

Shay left Philly that Friday morning. She caught the first Amtrak train smoking headed to New Carrolton, Maryland and took a cab to his office. He had given her one of his business cards, and she planned to visit him at his office. He couldn't avoid her *there*.

Linden was the CEO of Stewart International, an office supply company. Shay had every intention of seeing him *that* day. But if he chose to ignore her again, a sistah would have to come out of her face, and *everyone* in his company would *know* about their little secret!

Three hours later, Shay stepped into his office dressed in a conservative navy blue pantsuit and gold tank top.

"May I help you?" An elegant, matronly woman sitting behind a desk stamping envelopes for outgoing mail asked.

"Yes, I'd like to see Mr. Stewart," Shay said politely.

"Do you have an appointment?" She asked, smiling up at Shay.

"No, I don't, but he'll see me. My name is Shay Bennett."

"I'm sorry, Ms. Bennett, but Mr. Stewart is out of the office for an extended period of time. Would you like to see his vice president of sales, Mr. Chandler? He's handling all of Mr. Stewart's clients."

"Yes, I'll speak with him, instead."

Mr. Chandler turned out to be the blond-haired suit—one of the men with Linden at the club in St. Lucia. He was working out of Linden's office, she noted, as she stepped into the office. Linden's name was boldly embossed across the door.

"Where's Linden?" Shay demanded the moment the secretary closed the door. She marched up to the desk with a serious attitude.

"He's out on medical leave. May I help you?" he asked, politely. There was a smug look on his face as if he was covering for Linden.

"Why don't you *cut* the *bullshit?* He was fine the last time I saw him. I'm not leaving this office until I see him!" she announced.

"You're in for a *long* wait because he's *not* in the building. How may I help you?"

He asked, sitting high and mighty behind the desk in Linden's office.

"Do you *remember* me?"

~ 79 ~

"Yes, you created *quite* a show at that club in St. Lucia, Ms. Caramel Delight. Peter and I had bets on you, and I betted that you'd make it with the boss."

"My name is Shay Bennett, and I really need to see him. Don't *make* me create a scene in here."

He stared at her for several seconds.

"I'll plant myself in this office until I received what I came for," she threatened.

Finally, he gave her what she wanted.

"Linden was in a car accident on his way home from the Baltimore/Washington International Airport, returning from St. Lucia. There was a head-on collision with a tanker truck, and now he's recuperating at his parents' home in Virginia."

Panic, like Shay never known before, tightened her throat.

"H-how badly was he hurt?"

"He's *paralyzed*, Shay."

"No!"

Her chest felt as if it would burst, and she collapsed in the first chair nearest to her. Tears rolled down her cheeks. Now, she knew *why* she hadn't heard from him. He really wasn't avoiding her.

He needs me!

"I need to see him. Please…may I have his parents' address?"

"Linden isn't receiving visitors, Shay."

"He'll see *me!*"

"You were *just* an island fling, Shay. You can't possibly believe Linden was serious about your relationship?"

"That's none of your *damn* business! I'm not leaving this office until you give me their address."

"I'll call security," he countered.

"Call them, and then *everyone* in this company will know about my relationship with Linden," she added, sweetly.

"You're *quite* a bitch when you don't get your way."

Shay didn't back down. "Give me his parents' address, and I'll need a car to take me there!"

§

The Lincoln Town Car entered a winding driveway pulling in front of a mansion, in Shay's opinion.

Damn, Linden comes from money, and this house is impressive, she thought.

A corner property, beautifully landscaped lawn with burgundy and white bricks, spilt-level ranch house, attached garage, and a gazebo that sat on a half acre of land. Shay was indeed impressed.

A cold knot formed in Shay's stomach as she waited for the front door to open. It felt like she had been standing there forever. There was a silver Bentley and a navy blue Lexus parked in the driveway, so someone *had* to be home. A middle-aged, woman of color, who appeared to be annoyed by her presence, opened the front door as Shay rang the doorbell for the third time.

"H—hello, may I see Linden?" Shay inquired, her stomach churning with anxiety.

"Linden's sleeping, and he's not receiving visitors," she said puckering her upper lip. Her doe colored eyes seemed to stare right through Shay.

The woman gave her the once-over.

"Ma'am, I took the train all the way from Philly to see him. When I stopped by his office, Chandler informed me of the accident, and he hired a car to bring me here. Please...may I wait for him to wake up?"

"Natalie, let the girl in," a familiar-sounding voice called out.

Reluctantly, the woman opened the front door wide enough for Shay to slip through and she saw him from the foyer. Linden was the spitting image of his dad.

"Mr. Stewart, I apologize for just stopping by unannounced like this, but I just found out about Linden's accident. I was hoping I could see your son."

"Please, come in and have a seat."

On trembling legs, Shay nearly collapsed on the deep red sofa cushion grateful for something steady and solid to hold her weight. Nervous, she pulled at the hem of her suit jacket. She tried to play it cool—as if she normally hung out with white people.

"Did I hear you say you arrived from Philadelphia?"

"Yes, sir. I took the train out this morning."

"You never told us your name!" That arrogant woman exclaimed, a sarcastic tone in her voice.

For a maid, that woman is rude and outspoken. Mr. Stewart must have given her free reign in running his home, Shay thought.

"I'm sorry; where are my manners? My name is Shay Bennett."

Mr. Stewart and that annoying woman stared daggers at one another. You couldn't miss the message in their eyes.

"Natalie, bring our guest a glass of your delicious, sweet tea. I would like a glass as well," Mr. Stewart added.

She opened her mouth, and then closed it as she stomped out of the room mumbling something under her breath.

"How do you know my son?" he asked politely.

His tone continued to be warm and friendly. She heard that same warmth in his son's voice. Linden had his father's height, muscular build and sparkling violet eyes.

For a man who is at least sixty years old, he's still handsome... charming—which he passed onto his son.

"We met a month ago when he was in St. Lucia on business," Shay said, having the feeling he already knew that.

Natalie returned to the living room with three glasses of iced tea on a sparkling silver serving tray. She handed each of them a glass. After taking her first sip, Shay agreed that the tea *was* delicious.

Shay hadn't eaten anything that morning, so her stomach chose that *exact* moment to churn. She was embarrassed by the sound of her stomach growling—telling on her. Both of them heard it.

"Would you like something to go with that tea, Shay? We've just had lunch, and there's *still* some leftover shrimp salad," Mr. Stewart offered.

"Please, if you don't mind."

The shrimp salad, along with a garden salad, was *just* what she needed to soothe her empty stomach. Mr. Stewart and Natalie sat quietly while Shay ate her lunch—watching, and communicating with their eyes, again. If she didn't know better, she'd say *something* was going on between those two.

Did Mrs. Stewart know about them? Shay wondered.

~ 83 ~

"That was delicious. Thank you for the meal, Natalie."

"Would you like some more shrimp salad? I hate to see a hungry child."

"No, I'm fine, now. I left home early this morning, without eating anything."

"You were telling us how you met Linden," Natalie pressed her.

"How's Linden doing with his recovery?" Shay asked, purposely changing the subject.

"He's paralyzed from the waist down. After the accident, the doctors believed the swelling around the spinal cord was causing the paralysis. But since then, the swelling has reduced. Linden needs to start exercising his leg muscles, but he refuses to work out with the therapist," Mr. Stewart stated.

"No, that's *not* true, our son is feeling sorry for himself, and this pity party has to *stop*. He's wasting valuable time—time that he may not be able to get back after he comes to his senses," Natalie added, anger evident in her voice.

"*Excuse* me?"

"That's right; you heard me correctly. I'm Linden's *mother!*"

"Ahh—" Shay was momentarily speechless.

"Natalie, I believed you've shocked, Shay," Mr. Stewart said, smiling lovingly at his wife.

Shay's eyes slid over Natalie Stewart's body for a second time. She was about five-foot-one, had toffee colored skin, doe brown eyes, and dark brown hair with streaks of silver—which she wore in a short, sassy style. Her hair feathered her round shaped face. She was a very attractive woman when she smiled as she was now doing. There was nothing of Linden in her.

Hell yeah, this is a surprise!

"Linden never told me his mother was African-American," Shay added.

"Well, I guess you don't *know* my son as *well* as you thought," she countered, her tone dripping with sarcasm.

"I *know* he's the father of my unborn child," Shay volleyed, not thinking before she revealed that bit of information. Hell, she wasn't afraid of his mama.

"You *expect* us to *believe* you're carrying my son's child," Natalie quipped.

"I don't *care* if you believe me! Time will tell."

"We...no, I demand a paternity test on that child!"

"Natalie, stop this! Linden's health is more important, right now."

"She's *just* a *fling*, David — an island fling — and nothing more!"

"That's *not* for you to decide, sweetheart! Let Linden handle his own business. The young man is thirty-five years old, now. He's *no* longer your baby."

"He'd always be my baby!" she countered, glowering at her husband.

"I'm sorry; please...I shouldn't have said anything about the baby. I just want to see Linden."

"This is a *good* thing. Linden needs to refocus. You're just what we need to shake up our son," Mr. Stewart added.

Natalie and Shay looked at one another, giving him a "what do you mean" stare.

"What do you mean by *that*, David?"

"We've both heard Linden cry out Shay's name in his fretful sleep. Evidently, she's *important* to our son. He's afraid he'll no longer be able to share intimacy with

~ 85 ~

a woman. Shay can prove to him that he's not dead below the waist. She should seduce him. The news of their child will motivate him to start rehabilitation."

"David? Hmm, I *do* see your point. This *could* work."

She turned toward Shay. "Will you help save our son?" Natalie surprisingly inquired.

"I love Linden. Whatever he needs, I'll give him."

"He's going to fight you every step of the way," Mr. Stewart said, sharpness in his tone.

"I believe she can handle him. Shay didn't back down from *me*," Natalie added.

"No, she most certainly did not." Mr. Stewart chuckled at his wife. "It will be interesting to watch the two of you together. I see now why my son was attracted to you. Shay—you're beautiful, and not afraid to fight for what you want. Those are the same qualities, I see in my wife—who can be over-protective of her *only* son. Natalie doesn't realize that she *won't* always be first in *our* son's heart. That is something she will have to face—sooner than she anticipated."

"We will see, David," Natalie countered. She would have to prove herself worthy of their son.

Shay gave them a tentative smile.

"When do we start?"

"No time like the present. In fact, sweetheart, we should leave them alone. Let's get a room at the Marriott. That way Linden won't be able to involve us when he doesn't get his way, if we're not here," David added.

"*Wait!* You're really going to leave me alone with him?"

"You can handle him, *sugar*," Natalie's voice now dripped like honey. "After all, you claimed you conceived a child together." She trailed her husband, leaving Shay alone in their living room.

"But—I...Okay girl, you can *do* this. Show the man how much you love him," Shay said to the empty room convincing herself she could.

Chapter Ten

Shay eased into Linden's bedroom and found the curtains were drawn. Barely any light seeped through the window. She could make out his body under the blanket while she quietly stripped out of her clothes. She eased into the bed without waking him, and she watched him sleep.

Hmm, his scent is just as I remember, she thought.

His body's warmth eventually lulled her to sleep.

§

When Shay's eyes fluttered open, she found her head resting on Linden's chest. Her fingers were caressing his left arm, and their legs were intertwined.

"What are you doing here?" His voice was thick and unsteady.

She eased off his chest, and found he had turned on the bedroom light. A remote control switch lay on the nightstand. She was also shocked to see the after-effects from the accident. Although it had been a month since the car accident, he *still* had bruises and discoloration on his face.

"Ahh, babe, look at you. Why didn't you *call* me?" She whispered, gently touching the bruises so close to his now dull eyes. Thank God, he could still see.

"I don't want your *pity*, Shay!"

"I love you!"

"Why are you in my bed, undressed like this?" Linden bellowed, as he tried to shove her off his body.

"I want to *hold* you."

"I can't satisfy you in *that* way! Didn't my parents tell you I'm paralyzed?"

"How do you know you *can't* make love to me? Let's try."

"Get out of my bed *and* this house, Shay! I can't *believe* my mother allowed you into my bedroom."

"Why didn't you tell me your mother was African-American?"

"I thought I'd surprise you. But that doesn't matter, anymore. What we had is *over*."

"So, I was *just* an island fling to you?"

"Yes!" he raged, balling his hand in a fist. She couldn't miss the anger in his voice.

"And this has nothing to do your being paralyzed, now?"

"No!" he barked.

Shay couldn't help but see his vulnerability. A lone tear slid down his cheek when he turned his head away from her.

"Don't be afraid. God won't put too much on *our* shoulders that we can't handle. Lean on me, and let my love strengthen you. Can I hold you?" she whispered, with much love in her tone.

Shay laid her head back on his chest. His heartbeat throbbed against her ears.

"Do you remember that day we climbed the Petit Piton Mountain, and I made a big fuss?"

"Yes," he mumbled fighting the scent of her, as well as how much he loved and missed her.

"Well, I was really afraid, Linden. You see, I had a fear of heights, but I couldn't reveal that to you. Even then, I knew that I loved you. My love for you pushed me up that mountain."

"I never noticed your fear, Shay."

"You cured me that day."

"This is different, Shay…"

"No, it isn't," she cooed. Lovingly, her eyes caressed his face. "You remember afterwards, when we made love in the Piton waterfall and you didn't use a condom? We made a baby."

Linden stared into her eyes, surprised by what she revealed—but not really since they had unprotected sex, many times that week. *I was reckless—something I had never done with a woman,* he thought.

Shay took his left hand and placed it across her stomach. "Our baby is growing inside of me, *we* need you."

"I'll have my father write you a check. How much do you want—one, two thousand a month, Shay?"

"I don't want your *damn* money!"

"Isn't that why you're here? You claim that baby is mine!"

Shay balled up her fist. That was the only thing preventing her from smacking Linden in the face.

"Tell me, you don't love me, Linden, and I'll walk right out of that door!"

"I-do-not-love-you, Shay!" he with as much sincerity he could muster.

"You're not going to piss me off. I'm not walking away!"

Tears slid down Shay's cheeks. She kissed his mouth passionately, silencing his last words, but his lips were stiff and defiant—until he stopped fighting his desire. Then, he swept her tongue inside of his mouth. Their tongues danced and curled, but then her needs were heightened. Her tongue slid down his body, licking, tasting, kissing, *every* part of him, and she left the *best* for last.

As she got closer to his release, Linden fought her every step of the way. He tried to buck her body off his; but then, her lips tasted from the head of his cock—massaging him. Her right hand palmed his family jewels, and she massaged them tenderly, while her mouth worked his sex. Eventually, she felt his defenses weakening, and nature took control of his body, causing a response—he thickened and swelled within her moist, warm mouth.

Shay straddled his hips, and with Linden's help, guided his erection inside her dewy vagina. Tenderly, she made love to the man who held her heart within the palms of his hands. He was the father of her unborn child! Together, they both cried out from their second orgasm.

§

"I love you, Shay, and *our* baby. Thank you!"

"You're welcome."

She gazed into his sparkling eyes that no longer held pain, but were now filled with tears. "I know you love me, Linden!"

Linden wiped his eyes, choked by the emotions overwhelming him.

He grabbed her star diamond pendant gracing her long, sleek neck.

"I love my present. Thank you."

He pulled her to his chest and hugged her tight.

Shay felt the thundering of his heart pounding against her breasts, and she held him—caressing his moist back.

"It's okay, babe," she cooed, until Linden had his emotions back in check.

§

"You're so sure of yourself, Shay, because you've managed to get me hard, and my seed flowing again." He chuckled.

"My love for you did that, Linden."

"I can't live without touching your satiny skin." Linden's fingers slid down her ass; his sex still buried within her softness, and his seed flowing between them. "And, I can't live without this, Shay—being inside of your warmth, our bodies as one," he confessed.

"You don't have to live without that…us, Linden. I'm not going anywhere."

"You'll have to give up your job, Shay."

"It's just a paycheck," she grinned back at him.

"Move to Baltimore, Maryland."

"Done!"

"Marry me!"

"When?"

"Tomorrow?"

"Linden! I need a little more time."

"Okay, I'm not being realistic. As soon as I can make the arrangements," Linden stated with certainty.

His thumb teased her full lips.

Their eyes locked. There was so much love in them.

"There's a ring to match that star pendant. I commissioned the designer to make it: your engagement ring."

"I'm sure I'll love it, too."

Her emotions were rippling.

"Where are my parents?"

"They've checked into a hotel."

"That had to be my father's suggestion."

"He wanted to give us some time alone."

"And my mother went along with that?"

"Yes…eventually, she agreed," Shay groaned.

The stroking of his fingers sent pleasant jolts throughout her body. Instinctively, her body arched toward him. Linden swelled, and once again stretched her vaginal walls.

"You're ready for round two, my future wife, Mrs. Linden David Stewart?"

"Shouldn't you rest?"

"No!"

"We need to inform your doctor on your change in condition. I don't want to hurt you."

"Hurt me…hurt me, sweetheart. I *want* you to hurt me. I can feel your hands stroking my legs, feel your love muscles clenching me, and I've never felt better!"

His tongue demanded full surrender, and she met the full force of his passion with an equal force of her own.

Chapter Eleven

Four months later

Shay and Linden were married in a private ceremony on an exceptionally warm October day, in the garden of Linden's parent's Virginia home. Shay's parents were deceased so her two first cousins, Nia and Tatiana, escorted her down the aisle toward the redwood gazebo, where Minister Vernon, Linden, and his best man, Chandler, stood.

The leaves were gold, brown, and burnt orange. Her cousins wore tea length satin, teal green dresses. Their matching cropped jackets were edged with black fur. The radiant bride wore a sleeveless, off-white chiffon dress and a white mink jacket, which concealed her delicate condition.

In front of a hundred guests, the bride and groom expressed their unconditional love for one another.

Linden turned to their family and friends and started to share some intimate details of their Caribbean love affair.

"Shay," Linden said, smiling lovingly down at her as he took her hands within his. "For the past year and a half, I thought all I wanted in my life was to make my father and grandfather proud of me. Being the CEO of Stewart International was an honor to me. It gave me the challenge I needed: working for the family's business, making it better than when my grandfather started the company. It motivated me to reduce expenses and increase profit. I strived to bring in new business. I love working for the company, but it's not my whole life. On a business trip, and after landing the biggest deal since I took over the reign of the company, I met a woman. She was breathtakingly-sensuous, and I was mesmerized. She invited me on the dance floor and blew my mind with that luscious body of hers. We danced, I invited her back to my suite, and we spent the *most* amazing seven days together. When I left the island, I knew you were the woman I didn't know I'd been searching for."

"I gave you a star diamond pendant and commissioned the designer to make the matching diamond ring—possibly, as an engagement ring. On my way home from the airport, I was thinking about you and not on driving my Hummer. I hit a tanker truck and thank God I was alive, but I found myself paralyzed. I thought I had lost you forever."

"A month later, I was still having a pity-party, until you came to me, and brought me back to life. Shay...you gave me back my manhood—and the ability to walk again. I love you, with all of my heart and soul. I love our baby you carry within your womb," he declared proudly, and his hands caressed her slightly rounded belly.

§

"And, you hold my heart within the palms of your hands," Shay whispered, breathlessly nearly speechless by all he had said.

She gazed into his smoldering eyes, and revealed to him something she had meant to tell him before then.

"St Lucia…I fell in love with the island three years ago. I returned with a man I thought loved me. He disrespected me on the second day of our trip. I'd saved every penny to make that romantic getaway, but I wasn't going to allow him to spoil the rest of my vacation. I dressed brazenly that evening and went to The Pulse Club.

"You, along with two men clad in business suits, sauntered into the club. After drinking three rum punches, I was bold that night, and I sashayed over to your table, and invited you to dance with me. On the dance floor, I gazed into your eyes, and fell in love for the first time in my life. Not only did I fall in love with your striking violet eyes. I loved your passion, your generosity both in and out of bed, your warm and giving soul, and our baby we created together. There is *no* me *without* you, Linden," she said. Tears coursed down her cheeks.

"I love you, sweetheart," Linden repeated.

He wiped her warm tears away and he kissed her deeply, disregarding the minister and their guests as their passion for one another consumed them.

Nia and Tatiana wiped their own eyes, moved by their cousins' love for Linden.

Chandler smiled across at his best friend who had *truly* found love on the island of St. Lucia. His eyes raked over Tatiana Edwards' petite body. She was a strikingly beautiful, passionate woman, and he had every intention of getting to know that passionate side of hers.

Minister Vernon wiped his teary eyes with his hankie, touched by their exchange. He'd never married a couple more in love with one another, and he cleared his throat for the second time. He was ready to continue with the traditional vows.

Tears of joy slid down Natalie Stewart's cheeks. She had never seen Linden as happy as he was at that moment. He boldly repeated after Minister Vernon, "With this ring, I promise..." In five months, she'll be holding her *first* grandchild in her arms, and she and David were counting the days. She thought, as she witnessed the ecstatic couple she fastened her eyes on her husband.

David's eyes left his son's to shine upon his wife's face. Natalie was just as beautiful today, as she had been when they were married over thirty-eight years, ago. In the beginning of their marriage, it had been hard on them. Both Natalie and his parents were against the marriage. They couldn't possibly believe their white son was in love with an African-American woman, and vice versa, but their love for one another was strong. They didn't allow their parents' negativity to stop them from getting married.

After Linden was born, their parents relented and started to visit their home. He knew they wanted to see their grandson, and to be a part of his life. Then, they started to attend Sunday dinners, and on Linden's first

Thanksgiving and Christmas holiday, both of their parents' showed up with food and gifts as if it had been the norm. His eyes slid over to their mothers. Tears slid down their cheeks, and they were holding hands. David thought he would never see this day. Thank God, his son would have the support of *all* of his family, something they didn't have in the beginning of their marriage. He was a man with wealth, in fairly good health, and had the love of his life sitting right beside him. Life was looking good.

David reached out and took Natalie's left hand and tenderly kissed her ring finger. Violet eyes sparkling with tears now, gazed down into happy doe colored brown eyes.

Natalie's tear-filled eyes flamed with desire for her husband of thirty-eight years.

"I love you!" he mouthed.

She squeezed his hands and returned the sentiment.

§

Linden's parent's wedding gift to the couple was a two-week stay on the island of St. Lucia. They would honeymoon at the Jade Mountain Resort, and in the same suite they fell in love—The Star Infinity Pool Suite.

For eight blissful days, the Stewarts hold up in their suite—making love, dining on the resort's finest cuisine, and making love again and again, until they *finally* returned to the real world.

That evening, Shay wasn't feeling nausea, and she wanted to go dancing at The Pulse Club. The striking couple, clad in navy blue and tangerine, had just stepped out of the resort's elevator when they were approached by an older, distinguished, looking gentleman.

"Mr. and Mrs. Stewart, I'm Robert Carlton, manager of the Jade Mountain Resort. Are you and your wife enjoying your stay?" he inquired.

Linden shook his hand. "Yes, we are, sir. This is our second stay in the Star Infinity Pool suite, by the way. We were here in May. My wife and I wouldn't spend our honeymoon *anywhere* else," Linden declared.

"It's nice to know that you chose to return to our resort. We're proud of our little piece of heaven, here at the Jade Mountain Resort. I just wanted to let you know the Stewarts have broken the record for the number of days a couple has stayed confined in their suite. The record was five days. I'd like to present you with a plaque, and a thirty percent discount off of your next visit to our resort. With your permission of course, the resort's photographer would like to take your photo, and we'd like to display it in our lobby—along with our other guests. You'll have to sign a release, and we could set up a time and place at your convenience," he said in a mouthful mesmerized by Mrs. Stewart's beautiful eyes.

"Sweetheart, we've broken the record," Linden repeated. His violet eyes shimmered as he gazed down at his gorgeous wife.

Shay was unaware of the captivating picture she made in a simple tangerine sundress. It fit snugly, and the color illuminated her already glowing caramel-colored skin. Impending motherhood certainly agreed with her, along with Linden's tender loving care.

He grabbed Shay's left hand and kissed her wedding ring. "I promised my sweetheart, we'd go dancing tonight; otherwise, we'd still be inside of our suite. I'm going to give my mama-to-be whatever she wants. It's debatable if we conceived this bundle of joy right here in your resort or under the Piton waterfall," he stated with pride, as his hands circled her extended waistline.

"This is a beautiful resort, Mr. Carlton. I fell in love with my husband here, and we'd be delighted to take that photo. We intend to come back for our second anniversary, and maybe we'd break our own record!" She winked at Linden.

Shay, lovingly stared into her husband's shimmering violet eyes. She was happier than she'd ever been, and looked forward to a lifetime of happiness with Linden and their child.

The End

*Author's Note

Scenes in this book are based on the St. Lucia Jazz Festival that took place on May 2-11, 2008. The author took creative license in depicting the events of the ten-day concert.

And the saga continues…

A preview of my upcoming release, Drop It Like It's Hot, Seduction Series, Book Two, Tatiana and Chandler's erotic ride.

Book Blurb

Drop It Like It's Hot

The moment interior designer Tatiana Andréa Edwards gazes into Thurston Taylor Chandler's Caribbean-blue eyes at her cousin's wedding, she knows she wants to get to "know" him in the biblical way. He drops it like its hot inside of the gazebo; and six months later, she can't deny she wants another connection.

Chandler can't forget the passionate woman whose body feels like home to him. Tatiana returns to Maryland for her cousin Shay baby's christening. Now that they share a goddaughter, he doesn't waste time making his intentions clear. The moment they're reunited, they can't keep their hands off one another. As love blossoms, a past mistake could tear them apart.

Will Tatiana be able to right her wrong before Chandler's former fiancée, Marcella Bradley, gets her man back?

Drop It Like It's Hot

Prologue

October 8, 2010, Virginia

Tatiana Andréa Edwards sat to the right of her cousin and best friend, Shay Bennett, at a swanky French restaurant. They were attending the rehearsal dinner for Shay and her fiancé, Linden David Stewart.

Linden closed down the 5-star restaurant to have a private party. The best man, Thurston Taylor Chandler Jr., (everyone called him by his last name, Chandler), had just offered up a toast to the happy couple.

Shay looked exquisite in a simple navy blue sheath dress. The dress accentuated her caramel skin. Her ebony curls were piled on top of her head and ringlets of curls graced her forehead and the nape of her neck. Her hazel eyes welled up with tears. They spilled down her flushed cheeks from the eloquent words spoken by Chandler. There was a radiance on her face—an afterglow from being in love—and her impending pregnancy certainly agreed with her. Shay met and fell in love with Linden, on the island of St. Lucia. Their passion for one another created the baby she was carrying. They were to be married tomorrow afternoon in the garden of Linden's parents' Virginia home.

Tatiana was mesmerized as she watched the blond, blue eyed Chandler take his seat to the left of Linden. She had to admit that for a white boy, he wasn't bad looking. In fact, he was downright gorgeous. He stood at six-feet-one, dressed in a blue Armani suit, which brought out the color of his eyes. The suit fit his body to absolute perfection. His broad shoulders, washboard abs, and muscular arms and thighs screamed sex. Tatiana wanted to touch and stroke him everywhere. When he spoke, his voice was deep. His southern drawl was proper, yet his words held nasty overtones. She was turned on by him even more; and when his intense looking orbs scanned over her body, she was a goner.

The first time they met, over two months ago, he shook her right hand as if she were a business associates. Tatiana felt a current of electricity radiate down her body slowly until it settled within her feminine core. His eyes—the blue-green color of the Caribbean ocean—made her want to dive in and try the water.

Tatiana wasn't usually attracted to white men. She believed in dating her black brothers, and had in fact chewed Shay's ears off about her choice. Shay had told her, "You don't fall in love with a color, but in love with a man." She had to admit, Linden was as fine as hell, and very much in love with her cousin.

Why not date a white man?

The way Tatiana's body heated up every time Chandler was near made her reconsider her earlier decision.

§

"You may kiss your bride," Minister Vernon announced.

Not a dry eye was seen when Tatiana's tear-filled eyes scanned the wedding guests in the venue. Linden and Shay both revealed intimate details about their Caribbean love affair, which left the family and friends breathless.

Chandler's eyes locked on Tatiana. He sent her a hidden message of desire—want: pure and simple. His eyes traveled down her tea-length, teal green dress which flattered her shapely petite body. It brought out the golden-honey hues of her skin, and the rich auburn luster of her hair. Her hair was swept up in a cluster of large curls on top of her head. The green flecks in her hazel orbs sparkled and enticed him. Her diamond stud earrings and matching pendant sparkled against the rays of the sun when she turned her head back to the gazebo.

Tatiana was unaware of the captivating picture she made when she smiled.

Seductively, Chandler winked at Tatiana; and demurely she looked away, but her pulse raced.

For the rest of the ceremony, Tatiana subtly glanced over at Chandler—zeroing in on his classic golden boy features. She couldn't stop looking at him. He was dressed in a black tuxedo, teal-colored cumberbund around his waist, and a matching teal scarf tucked inside his left breast pocket. He looked sinfully handsome, like eye candy.

Chandler's skintone was bronzed from his recent vacation to the Dominican Republic. His thick, tawny-gold crew cut was gelled and slicked back away from his forehead. It called attention to his face, his long angular nose, his sinfully long, thick golden eyelashes, firm chin, and his sensuous lips. He was hot! He kept licking his lips as if they were dry, but to Tatiana's eyes, they were fiery, yet, moist, full and trembling—like a beacon—inviting and beckoning her.

He is forbidden territory, yet I want a taste, she thought.

After the ceremony, the guests were led inside for champagne and hors d'oeuvres, while the wedding party and the immediate families posed for photos in the garden.

Eduardo, the original photographer, known for capturing the essence of any occasion, was hired to photograph the Stewart nuptials. His sudden illness caused Linden's friend, Paul, to take over the job. They had been friends since high school and Shay had been in tears earlier because she wouldn't have any photographs to capture their special moments. Paul wasn't a professional, but everyone loved his photos, so he offered his services.

Tatiana thought he was an *asshole*. Paul's instructions were sometimes confusing. "Stand there, no stand here. Come closer, don't move, and give me your most dazzling smile." He irritated the hell out of her.

Paul took the usual photos: the bride and groom, the bride with her family, the groom with his family, and several photos with the entire wedding party. The family was finally released to enjoy the reception, while the wedding party stood back to take additional photos.

Oh no, not another photograph with just the wedding party! Tatiana wanted to scream.

During the taking of those photos, she stood beside Chandler and the bridal couple. Nia stood to the left of Linden and Shay, and Paul kept clicking away. The sudden caress on her ass had Tatiana bolting out of position. A pebble caught the heel of her right slingbacks, and she was falling.

Chandler came to her rescue. Effortlessly, he lifted Tatiana by the waist to prevent her from falling face down in the grass.

Surprised by Chandler's action and very much aroused, Tatiana's eyes lit up. Desire clawed at her, hot and sharp.

"Tatiana!" Paul's deep, booming voice grated on her nerves.

"Are you all right, Tatiana?" Chandler inquired as if he hadn't been the cause of her sudden tumble. The beginning of a smile tipped the corners of his sexy lips when he stared down at her.

Paul groaned. His frustration was mounting. "I'd like the maid of honor and the best man back in position, please!"

Tatiana's four-inch heels sank into the moist grass when she tried to take her position. Chandler, the perfect gentlemen, reached out a hand to assist her.

Every hormone in Tatiana's body sizzled when she stepped back into position.

"Would you move a little closer, Tatiana," Paul ordered.

Paul stared down at Tatiana, sucked his teeth, and then he adjusted the lighting before bringing the camera to his eyes. He stared into the camera lens. Tatiana was a beautiful woman, but she was also an ice princess, he thought, who worked his last nerve. She had just ruined the *best* shot of the day.

Tatiana moved closer as Paul had instructed.

Being naughty and appearing innocent, Chandler took full advantage and squeezed Tatiana's ass again as he smiled into the camera.

That time, she didn't react to his fingers groping her buttocks. A low moan slipped past her lips.

To Chandler's ears, her husky sound aroused him as no woman ever had.

"May I have a smile, Ice Princess?" Paul instructed, a sharpness in his tone then.

"I'm not an ice princess!" Tatiana fired back. "You're the most annoying wannabe photographer I've ever met. Linden needs to fire your ass!"

Paul growled.

"Tatiana, please, we're almost done. Then, you can get a drink and cool off," Nia added. She needed a drink as well.

The happy couple's eyes were locked onto one another. Stealing a kiss whenever they could, nothing disturbed their world.

Tatiana rolled her eyes at her sister and obediently fell back in line.

"You're not an ice princess, and I'm going to prove it," Chandler's low, disturbingly sexy drawl whispered into her ear.

She stared into his Caribbean Ocean-colored eyes and watched them shimmer. The wave she thought she saw in his eyes looked more inviting by the minute.

"Okay, just three more shots, and we can all take a break," Paul announced, backing into position as he brought the camera to his eyes.

Tatiana smiled into the camera and ignored the man who whispered in her ear. His hands and manly scent turned her body into quivering mush.

After the last shot, the wedding party was finally free to join the rest of the guests.

"Thank God," Nia groaned. "I would have melted another minute more."

Tatiana and Nia made a beeline to the bar.

The Stewarts set up a dais in front of their kidney-shaped swimming pool for the wedding party. Twelve round tables, draped in an elegant layout of teal and black, surrounded them. The servers matched the wedding party, attired in black pants and teal shirts. They worked quickly and efficiently to serve their guests. Anita Baker, Kenny G and Dionne Warwick songs serenaded the guests, and the liquor and food flowed generously. David and Natalie Stewart spared no expense to make this special day for their only son.

Tatiana's first glass of Chivas Regal, a twelve-year blend, had a honey flavor. It went down smoothly, but it didn't quench her thirst. She ordered another drink within one minute of finishing it. It was supposed to cool her off; instead, her body was inflamed.

"You want another drink, Beautiful?" the flirtatious bartender asked.

Tatiana's gaze slid up to his Emerald Green eyes, and she couldn't miss their smoldering depth. He took her right hand and discreetly drew circles on her palm, then squeezed her fingers.

"No, thank you." She wasn't in the mood and pulled her hand out of his grip.

"You want to get together, later?" he inquired, not picking up on her rejection.

"I have a man," Tatiana retorted. She stood and walked quickly away from the annoying bartender.

The reception was in full swing. Tatiana's family started a Soul Train lineup, and she watched the happy couple lead the way dancing down the center aisle—followed by his parents, her parents, her brother, and sister, cousins, and the rest of their crazy family. Tatiana wasn't in the mood for dancing. She hadn't seen Chandler since they sat down to dinner and he offered that eloquent toast.

Where is he? She wondered, looking around the room.

Her head started to hurt. Whenever she wore her hair pinned on top of her head for a long period of time, it would throb. She removed the pins in her hair, and shook her lustrous auburn curls out until they cascaded down her back. Barefoot, she appeared sexy and uninhibited as she slipped out of the patio door. The music was blaring, and she needed fresh air.

Tatiana went for a walk to clear her head. She headed in the direction of the gazebo. It was a beautiful and warm fall October evening. A soft breeze fanned her face and brushed against her thick curls. The sun had set. The crickets started chirping as the night life came alive. The grass felt cool against her bare toes. She took a deep breath and inhaled the numerous scents from the garden. Roses and the scent of jasmine filled the air, giving her a sense of tranquility. The throb in her head eased as she stared up at the night sky. The stars twinkled against the ebony sky. The sky embraced her as she extended her arms and twirled around, feeling young and carefree.

When Tatiana glanced back at the house, the candles flickered around the poolside; the Cha-Cha Slide music played, and she heard the cheers from inside of the house. She was happy for Shay, but she felt a little melancholy at the same time.

I want a man to love me the way Linden loves Shay.

The smell of tobacco permeated the air. Tatiana followed the scent until she found Chandler leaning against the entrance of the gazebo, with a cigarette in his left hand. She moved closer as if this moment were meant to be.

She was out there searching for him.

"May I have a puff?" Tatiana asked, inching closer.

"This is a nasty habit, Ana!"

"My name is *Tatiana*, remember?"

"I *like* Ana, it's *softer*. Now Tatiana is a bitch—a woman in heat." He said shocking her with his arrogance.

How dare you! Tatiana swung without thinking, but Chandler's reflexes were quicker. The cigarette butt was thrown in the grass. Tatiana found her hands behind her back, and his erection pressed into her ass.

"See, that is what I'm talking about." His voice was rough and close as he whispered into her sweet-smelling hair. "Tatiana needs to be in control. You're beautiful—absolutely, exquisitely beautiful. I came out here to get away from the allure of you. Why did you follow me, Ana?"

A crackle of energy passed between them. Hot. Raw. Carnal.

"What are you talking about?" She was angry that he pinned her hands behind her back, but was also aroused from the heat and smell of him. She knew exactly what he meant. *He feels it as well,* she thought.

"You've felt it since the very first day we met. The sparks, the dance, the chase; let's stop this."

He released her hands and swirled her around. They stood face-to-face. With eyes locked and smoldering, their bodies pressed dangerously close together and caused his loins to throb even more. He felt her shiver and smiled.

Chandler's hot, smoky breath blew into her face.

"Do you still want a puff, Ana?"

Without waiting for a response, his mouth descended and captured hers. His tongue darted across the seam of her moist lips until she opened them and allowed him inside. There was no "let's get to know one another," he knew what he wanted, and grabbed it.

Tatiana's eyes fluttered closed, and on a sigh, she gave in to the pleasure he offered. The sweet and subtle blend from the brandy he drank earlier filled her mouth, and combined with the menthol taste of the cigarette he just smoked.

Tatiana moaned, and he swallowed her passion.

Chandler's kisses were demanding and greedy as his tongue slid deeper into her mouth. He'd been hungry for a taste of Tatiana's lips for months. Silky and warm, he devoured her and couldn't get enough of her. His hands burned a path up her silky bare legs.

Tatiana felt the cool air against her ass when his fingers ripped her thong right off her hips. Seconds later, she tugged at his cumberbund, needing to feel the heat of their naked skin pressed together.

Chandler carried her inside of the gazebo for privacy, sat her on the edge of a lone table, and stepped out of his pants and boxer shorts.

Their eyes locked again as they intimately caressed one another.

Desire lit up his dreamy eyes. It clawed at her. His rock-hard erection pulsed and throbbed with the need of being surrounded by Tatiana. He tested her readiness and then drove between her moist thighs, deep and fast.

"*Hágame el amor,*" she cooed to him in Spanish.

Little did Tatiana know that Chandler spoke Spanish fluently. It was his second major in college. The language came to him effortlessly, and it became an invaluable tool for business. He had every intention of making love to her body as she cooed to him in her native tongue.

Seconds later, Tatiana's purr was sweet music to Chandler's ears and his body. She arched her hips to meet each thrust. Passionately, she matched him rhythm for rhythm as they made love with a hungry, feverish intensity. Her tea-length gown was gathered to her chest. He continued to pound into her sweet warm cunt. She wrapped her legs around his back to bring him deeper into her heat, smothering him with her clenching walls, and surrounding him with her feminine juices.

Chandler's lips and hard cock had Tatiana going buck wild in seconds. His skillful hands brought her body to the brink of an orgasm—so satisfying—so amazing that she had an outer body experience.

I am floating...My toes curl from the sweet sensation radiating down my body. I'm in my body, but out of my body. Looking on while experiencing every single ripple of heat and fullness, she thought.

"*Ay Papi,*" she cooed.

"T-a-t-i-a-n-a!" he groaned.

This is just too damn good — too damn delicious. I didn't know my own name could sound so sexy from Chandler's lips, she thought.

After their second round of lovemaking their hunger for one another finally abated.

Climatically wrapped in each other's arms they took deep breaths as their heartbeats slowly eased back to a normal pace.

Drop It Like It's Hot will be released in May 2012.

Tatiana Andréa Edwards has met her match: Thurston Taylor Chandler Jr. The novel is over 71,000 words. It will set up the rest of the books in the series. You can peek into Shay and Linden's lives and meet the rest of their dysfunctional family.

ABOUT THE AUTHOR

www.raewinters.com

The *Girlfriends Series* launched Rae's introduction into e-books. While she was at home taking care of her terminally ill father, she picked up her pen again and began to write.

Caribbean Heat is the first book in the Seduction Series. Rae is currently tweaking Tatiana and Chandler's erotic ride in *Drop It Like It's Hot* the second book in the series, where you can peek into the lives of Shay and Linden Stewart. It will be released in May 2012, first as a Kindle book and then in print.

Ms. Winters loves to hear from her readers. You can email her at raew154@gmail.com. Visit her online home: website at www.raewinters.com, Myspace at www.myspace.com/raewinters.com, and her blog at www.raewinters.blogspot.com.

Other works by Rae Winters

Red Rose Publishing
Salsa Heat

Available Now
Playing With Fire, Caribbean Heat, In My Sister's Footsteps, Another Chance, Incognito

Romance Series — *A Taste of Passion, Obsession, Undeniable*

Girlfriends Series — *Unfinished Business, Against My Will, Finding Love Again, Blindsided By Love*

Coming Soon *Time and Again, I'll Be There, Bittersweet Passion,* Book Three of the Seduction Series

Rae Winters Exclusive

Printed in Great Britain
by Amazon.co.uk, Ltd.,
Marston Gate.